To Avenge a Dead Glacier

TO AVENGE A DEAD GLACIER

Shane Tivenan

THE LILLIPUT PRESS
DUBLIN

First published 2025 by
THE LILLIPUT PRESS

62–63 Sitric Road,
Arbour Hill,
Dublin 7,
Ireland
www.lilliputpress.ie

Stories from this collection first appeared in the following journals:
'Dino Matcha', *The Stinging Fly*, Winter 2022; 'Whosever She Is
Is Beyond Me', *Eleven Stories, The Desperate Literature Prize
Anthology*, 2024; 'Mother vs Deep Blue', The Bridport Prize
Anthology, 2023; 'Honey Brown' *The Stinging Fly*, Winter 2023.

A CIP record for this title is available from The British Library.

Paperback ISBN 978 1 84351 917 1

eBook ISBN 978 1 84351 939 3

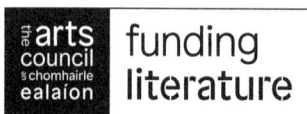

Lilliput gratefully acknowledges the financial support of the Arts
Council / An Chomhairle Ealaíon.

Set in 11.5 pt on 16 pt Sabon LT Std and Nouvelle Grotesk by
Compuscript
Printed and bound in Czechia by Finidr

To Bat and Mary

CONTENTS

DINO MATCHA

Dino Matcha's box flat is on the westside of Town.

Dino Matcha's Town is peopled by friend, family, foe.

Dino Matcha says the Town never got over that missed penalty against Milan in 1975. Heads dropped that day and never came back up.

Dino claims it's the want makes us weak.

Claims the government has a lot to answer for.

Claims governmental rent allowance for his one-bed box by the Shannon, and to the woman in the dole office he explains on a week-in, week-out basis that work of that description is for other sorts, the steady-as-you-goers, the nine-to-fucken-fivers, the three square meals and decide what's what aged early with hand-me-down opinions and plain sailing from childhood to confirmation to sweetheart marriage to 2.1 kids and fixed monthly payments and no questions asked, and that's just not Dino.

The woman looks blankly at her screen, week-in, week-out, tap tap tap tap tap, printout, hands Dino another Career Navigation appointment for the following week and says, Next.

Dino Matcha leans, whispers, Some days I don't know what to make of meself either, Mrs Killian, but I assure you this handout is a temporary measure. All I need is time to –

Next!

Dino Matcha puts it down to vested interests.

Says the flash floods of the mid-2000s – when the Town's sewers disembowelled themselves and entered front doors and floated out leather cushions from hire purchase L-shaped sofas and remote controls for plasma TV screens and instruction manuals for Jacuzzis, fucken Jacuzzis!, and carried it all off down the street – were no more than karmic bailiffs bringing warnings from somewhere deep that all was not well with the way we were living. The way we are living.

Dino Matcha, head in hands, says, No, no, no, there's enough mouths to feed in the world as it is, love. And off she goes.

Dino pushes his forehead again the cold bedroom wall and repeats over and over, Everything that leaves comes back.

Dino's box flat is close enough to the Shannon to hear its waters gushing through the sluices. He gapes daily at the river's flow. Says everyone from the Town knows people down there, such is the draw, such is the draw.

THE UNWANTED GAME

Charlie Clarence is of Scottish extraction, temper and complexion. He is Dundee United not Dundee. Says it is Godly grace what moves the legs of our most gifted strikers. Says if it wasn't for Ralph Milne's left peg, he'd never have had a son, and no cunt will ever tell him that it's not the Lord himself who orchestrates such events.

Charlie Clarence swears that fatherhood whipped him into shape. Blesses himself every time he passes the door of a boozer. Reckons that a club like Dundee United need not be winning more than one Scottish Premier League title in his lifetime, not after what happened in 1983. That the thought of the fire-in-the-wind-like movement of the crowd that day in the packed open stand behind the goal still goosebumps his skin. That he does not remember the one-night stand that cost him his marriage and gained him his son. That all he remembers of the day is this: Four minutes gone, I mean four fuckin minutes an how I'm even stood at that match is a story o the resurrection itsel. I've come to in a squat beh the docks. A beautiful young dame shakkin is awake an pointin to meh watch an handin is meh troosers an I canna lay claim to havin ever seen her afore. Inta the Smugglers an oor afore kick-aff an the rest o us are there – mortal. Blootered fae the night afore. I'm thinkin it's touch an go whether we'll even mak it the twenty minutes up the road – the camino the fuckin Santiago looks mair straight forward at that moment in time. But Reg, he rustles up some ching. There's naebidee else scorin ching in Dundee in the early 80s only oor Reg. So we single-file it to the bogs, pints in hands, nae time for discretion. Twa at a time inta the cubicle, pint knocked back beh the urinal, oot the fuckin door.

Now I lose the crew again in the approach to Dens Park, but at kick-aff – wutivir's brought us all there an wahivir's been left ootside an wutivir they've put in that fuckin ching that's burnin meh nostril – nane o that shite matters. Cause Dens Park might only be twa-hundred yairds awa fae oor home turf in Tannadice, but everybody in Dundee knows it's pure light-years that separate oor twa clubs.

An it's only four minutes on the clock an aff he goes. Ralphie Milne. Acquires the ball fae Luggy near the centre o the park. Turns to face the Dee's defence an they come oot hard but Ralphie, he's an absolute dancer. He dribbles. Shimmies. He's got Doddsy to the left an Billy Kirkwood oot on the right wing. Wi ah due respect to Doddsy, the man's left fut is for stannin on an no much else. An Ralphie often sade so himself that if he laid it aff to Billy Kirkwood on the right, the man wid've ended up hittin some puir cunt in Radio Tay. So he's no even lookin for any ither options as he's nearin Dundee's box. He's already visualized wut he's aboot to dae, cause like all the greats afore him, Ralphie studies form. He can read big Colin Kelly like a book – yih remember

Col do ya? Ayewiz fuckin fancied himself as the big lad. The only English man on the pitch that day an he's got the fuckin mooth to prove it. Likes to stand that extra metre aff his line an whisper a few sweet rough anes inta the ears o the opposition's strikers, shak thum up a wee bit. An Ralphie, number eight, jist a wee nick, a perfectly weighted chip wi his left peg an ower the keeper's hands an under the crossbar. A masterly opener. Four minutes later an we're twa up. Twelve months later an there's an Irish dame at the door talkin to the missus. This is Roy, she says, noddin in meh direction. It's his.

Dino Matcha calls it the unwanted game.

Charlie Clarence says we all get our comeuppance in the end.

SEE THE WANT

Charlie Clarence moves to Ireland in late 1984 to be close to his son. He has little money and no career but a taste for the page convinces him a night-time certificate in journalism is the way to go.

Dino Matcha receives his calling loud and clear, aged young, 1996. Picks up the paint can and sprays words onto depressed-looking walls, harmless embankments, burnt-out Opel Kadetts, factories reclaimed by nature, rotting school prefabs, butchered tree stumps, half-kicked-down fences, barriers, ramparts, rusted caravans, dumped washing machines.

Charlie Clarence is headbutted on the streets of the Town in 1989 and told to fuck back off across the water. His second meeting in St Mary's Hall on Northgate Street breaks him. On all fours he says, All I want to dae is rear meh son. I jist want to rear meh son like. At the fifth meeting he declares himself an alcoholic. Is told he's home. Takes a cup of tea. Starts to feel home. Begins the work.

Dino Matcha, everywhere he goes, sees the want.

Charlie Clarence lets on he doesn't see his teenage son crushing up prescription Tramadol and rolling up a note. He reverses out the bedroom door and shouts in, Cup o tea son? Aye, Da, go on. Sound son.

Dino Matcha says if you put your ear to the surface of the river and listen, eyes closed, you'll hear the swansongs of those swallowed by her over the years. But don't stay too close for too long – she's charismatic is the Shannon. She'll charm you in.

Dino Matcha is heavily armed against such charms. Graffiti can in hand. Montana. Ozo orange. Water based. Quick drying, as the rain's never far away. Molotow markers. SoySolv. Krink K-42s. Sprayer. Stencilled lettering in copperplate font. Dust mask. Latex gloves. And all weapons concealable inside his neon blue mack.

Charlie Clarence sits in the pub with his son. His hands never lost the shakes and he the guts of a decade off the gargle. Young Roy gets a taste for it nice and young. Pint an a nip son? Aye, Da, go on. Charlie assures his son that their blood is tangerine even though they live on the green isle. That he's going to upskill himself. Make enough money to fly them both to Dundee at the drop of a hat to watch games, and with fucken regularity at that, Are yih wi is son? Aye, Da. Listen, I'll be back in a sec – I just need me meds. Givin yih gyp son? Aye, Da. Charlie Clarence orders a pint and a nip for the wee man, and a coffee and a toasted sandwich for himself. He watches his son's gimped gait as he enters the jacks and turns to the barman and says, Funny, isn't it Bill? What's that, Charlie? How in the end, we all git oor comeuppance.

ALL OUR HATE

COMES HOME TO ROOST

Dino Matcha shows great promise as a young striker for St Peter's FC and makes the under-ten's number ten jersey his own at a mere eight years, two weeks old. Give him a ball and a yard of grass – writes Charlie Clarence for the *Athlone Observer* after witnessing a stellar performance at the Regional and District Schoolboy League Final of 1994 – and this kid will do damage.

Dino Matcha's lifetime ban from participating in any regional sporting event seems harsh at first for a fifteen-year-old, but not to the people who were at the match. The two-footed high-studded tackle on the Willow Park defender, long after the ball had left his feet, ended up being a career ender.

Your son has suffered extensive compound fractures to the tibia, fibula and patella of his left leg. The patella and quadricep tendons have also been severely ruptured. I'd prefer be given it straight like, Doc. If this was in my grandfather's day, Charlie, we'd be amputating the lower part of that leg. But with time and rehabilitation and medication, young

Roy will walk again, even run again, but chances are he'll do so with a limp.

WE MUST NOT HATE

WE MUST NOT HATE

WE MUST NOT HATE

The state developmental psychologist asks sixteen-year-old Donal McGowan why he doesn't fill in his CBT forms correctly. Cognitive behavioural therapy is not complicated, Donal. My name's Dino. Sorry, Dino, it's literally ABC. A, you write your activating event. B, your belief as to how this event will unfold. Then C, the key, you note the actual consequence of that event and how it aligns with your belief in B, and what we find time and time again is that B and C do not match up, therefore making A completely redundant as an activating event. What? We imagine things worse than they are, Donal. Dino. Dino, sorry, OK, so, imagine, A, you try to ring your friend and they don't answer. B, you believe your friend no longer likes you. C, a few days later they ring and say their phone was not working. But how? How what, Dino? How do we know they're telling us the truth?

Charlie Clarence attends his ten-year sobriety party. Cups of tea and Toffypops and whispers in his ear: This is no small feat, Chaz. Well done, Charlie. The young lad is proud, no doubt, Chazzer. We're all so proud of you here, Charlie.

Dino Matcha stops going to his CBT appointments and throws his medication in the bin. Says he's too young for therapy. Too young to be lying in bed all day listening to the sound of grinding teeth.

Charlie Clarence takes on shifts as a night cleaner in the regional college to pay for his master's. Writes for the *Westmeath Independent* during the day. Blesses himself every time he passes the door of a boozer.

Dino Matcha, no grub, low funds, gives in. Sits in the local job centre. Sickly grey ticket in hand. Six before him. Corporate slogans on the wall. Infinite. Linear. Growth.

Dino Matcha comes to his senses. Stands up. Leaves.

Shakes. Sprays. Seethes.

WANTED FOR CRIMES AGAINST HUMANITY:

RONALD MCDONALD, MICKEY MOUSE, ET AL.

Dino Matcha figures that if the true laws that govern us all are anything to go by, then linear growth can never exist: If you throw a stone in a straight line into space, throw it with enough force and wait enough time, that stone will come back to that exact hand. Fact. All movement happens in circles. Everything that leaves comes back. Zoom in on any circle in the world and you'll eventually hit straight lines. This information has always been hidden in plain sight – the pagan spirals, the snake eating its own arse. Everything we do comes back to visit us, tap tap tap on the shoulder, Hello there, remember me?

Roy Clarence survives another unintentional overdose. He awakes in the emergency room but is told he's being transferred to the drug and alcohol abuse section in the psychiatric ward.

Charlie Clarence smiles down at his son as he is trollied by orderlies through hospital corridors. I've jist got masel a master's son. Distinction. We kin branch oot now. Some freelance joab offers comin in arridee. Bills soarted on time fae now on an I'm gittin you that prevvit healthcare. We kin even treh ane o the new clinics, yih ken, ane o the fancy anes wah tak in all the celebs? Even Ralph Milne hud trouble wi the swally an pills son. It's nuhin to be ashamed o. But the drink made a mess o him. It wiz the drink that took Ralphie in the end. Are yih wi is son?

Dino Matcha, ear to the water, listens. Stays too close for too long and on him the Shannon works her charm.

Charlie Clarence gets young Roy on a back-to-work scheme as part of his social reintegration programme.

Dino Matcha takes off his shoes and socks. Places in a circle by the water's edge his phone, wallet, keys to the flat, spray paint, stencils, accoutrements, a picture of her, a picture of him and her, a wildflower. He drops his blue mack to the ground as he stands.

Roy Clarence limps off to his first day of paid work. His father fills up, chest out, mumbles to himself, If it wuzna for Ralph Milne's left peg.

Dino Matcha places his bare foot into the cold black body of the Shannon.

Roy Clarence places his hand on Dino Matcha's shoulder. Says, Sorry, pal, like, your work is bang on and that but I've got to repaint all these walls. New government scheme. Can't say I'm in complete agreement but powers that be and all that. Work is work. Need the money. Listen, pal, come out and I'll explain more. Take me hand there. The thing is, I know all the spots not on me list here. If you come out, I'll tell you where they are. I'll take you there. Come on. It's alright. Take me hand, pal.

Dino Matcha rocks and shivers back and forth on the banks of the river. Has his feet dried by young Roy Clarence. Has his socks and shoes put on as he tries to pull himself together.

Roy Clarence asks, Why?

Dino Matcha says, Such is the draw, such is the draw.

Roy Clarence says, Aye.

WHOSEVER SHE IS IS BEYOND ME

Pity lifts is all they offer me. Piss-take lifts from the young. Phones out sniggering ready to get a picture, but I walk by. That's what I do. I walk. I'm a walker. Their lifts I don't take. Left right left right head down hackles up. My dog Liam home alone drooling for the Pedigree in my bag. The little fairy girl, she's there as well. Making the odd appearance around the house. I have names for her but they flit and vanish before they stick.

I list things I can do as I walk. I can pull a good pint. Seed stitch a baby blanket. Handle whatever is thrown at me. The listing gets the thief out of my head. The thief in the white Hiace van, far side of the main road, eating his sandwich and drinking his tea and waving over from the forecourt of the petrol station. He has already today robbed me of my pension and one bag of messages. I can delouse any animal or man. Talk a plant out of dying. Tell by the clouds alone what sort of pain I'll have today. I'd like to stand in the town square and announce what I can do so they'll remember me, so they'll give me a good send-off when I go, but I can't. That's something for the other list – things I can't do. Speak in public. Work a crossword. Spoken sharp inside me in a voice I've never taken to, even though it's one of my own. Alice. That's the little fairy's name. The speed of her. Silver wings strapped to her back. Whosoever she is is beyond me.

The first car slows down wanting to be the hero. I look away into the ditch. Brambles, muck, coffee cups, clothes, a stringy condom that looks like an umbilical cord. A Reilly man used smuggle them down from Belfast during the ban. He sold them openly in the hotel bar. The car speeds off again. 212-RN. The bigger engines make me wince. I sometimes get the sensation I'm falling down out of myself, like does happen in dreams but I get it awake. That's the trouble with jumping from the roof of a barn – the feeling of falling never leaves you, even though I only jumped the once. And I young. And I working hotels. The child growing inside me.

A pain comes to my lower back, a fist of fire telling me a biblical shower is on the way. Coming in on the coat-tails of that north-westerly, the same wind that could lift nails from coffins, but I take it head-on. I let it sweep the thoughts from my mind. The umbilical the fairy the thief. My bunions and pains. The wind gives me something else to grapple with. I lean against it as I pass the turn for the hotel where I worked. Four mile left to home. Liam's Pedigree Vital in my left hand. The thief took everything else, the brazen bastard. Waiting in the corner of the post office smiling over and snatching my book from me before I got out the door and going straight back up and spending it at the counter. And they think I don't know they're all in on it. A crowbar wouldn't loosen my grip on that dog food. Alice is not that fairy girl's name. No Alice ever stood in my house.

The first drop of rain closes my eye like a slap. The next car pulls in on the hard shoulder up ahead. The barn I jumped from was a similar red. The corrugated sheets hot beneath my bare feet. I can make St Brigid's crosses from regular blades of grass. I can tell heath from heather. I can boil an egg to goo without a timer. The woman nudges her kids quiet and the husband tries fixing his smile, but I can tell a man who'll use the C word on me just by the shape of his face in a rear-view mirror. Hello ma'am, can we offer you a lift? I have a throatful ready and I hawk it up and spit it out as I pass. 241-MO. Nippy little turbo on it as it shoots off away from me. The thief across the road laughing and shaking his finger to not be doing that. I give him the fist, tell him to clear off. He laughs harder. I stare him down and his smiley face soon falls asunder.

The rain takes off proper, my can't-do list with it. Control my temper. Get away from this thief. Remember clearly what it's all about. Things I'll never master and what about it. Know thyself, some lad said once, but I never heard him say fix thyself. It's the sort of rain the road engineers couldn't even predict and it stays blanketed over the surface of the N61. The thief crosses and drives the Hiace up behind me. Flashers on. Tour de France job. I know what he's at. When you walk places you learn everything, you see all sorts. I saw a woman devour a roast-chicken dinner in the driver's seat outside Daly's at a roadworks traffic lights. Phone in hand like she at the kitchen table. Gone like Schumacher once green. A man with a towel on the steering wheel two cars up, different day, same lights. Going at himself good and hard and it broad daylight. Wouldn't even put it away and I walking by. I received a half-eaten Supermac's snack box to my temple as I walked home one Saturday evening. Scattered condiments on the road behind me. My hair smelt of curry sauce for days. Cars change people, that's my conclusion. Wrap a bit of steel around them and put a few rubber tyres underneath and you'd swear you'd made them untouchable. You see it all when you walk. You miss nothing. I've never even sat in an automobile. I'll walk to my own funeral before they get me into the back of a hearse.

A neat Powers and a brandy and Baileys while he waited for his Guinness to settle was what the principal liked to drink in the hotel bar. He was a different animal once he had a half day done on the high stool. He took to giving me lifts home after my shifts, the back of the Merc as big as the pantry in the home place. It was only when he climbed back into the front seat and I caught his eye in the rear-view mirror did I see what he really thought of me. He'd never let his guard down, though. Never once let the word slip from his lips, as close as he often came to spluttering it out. No father's name on the birth cert as agreed. Lump sum paid in full, but people grew funny around me when it happened.

I could name no father, no ring on my finger. They still act funny now even though there's no one left would remember the goings-on back then.

That principal got some send-off after the brain haemorrhage toppled him onto the floor of the bar. Same hotel. Same high stool. Big spread in the *Herald*. When they had him down in the ground I walked over with a mouthful ready, but I couldn't bring myself to spit it out. I was too quiet in myself, perhaps he wasn't worth it. But I reared that child as if I were two people. The summers so warm and long back then. I thought the heat from the corrugated sheets would burn straight through the soles of my feet if I didn't jump.

Mam, the thief shouts at me. Inching up the hard shoulder behind. I'm not your mother, I tell him over my shoulder. That's enough for today, Mam. Get in. You'll catch your death. It's nothing to what I'd catch in there beside you, I tell him, and he roars laughing at this. Not the most unpleasant laugh I've ever heard. Like the principal's but nicer. Soberer. I pay him no heed. I walk on.

*

I come to in the front of the Hiace. I must have fell down out of myself again. Some get carried off to the pearly gates in horse-drawn gold-studded carriages. Or St Michael rows them ashore on his boat of light, hallelujah. I get carted off in a white Hiace, a straight 2 litre, not even turbo. Joe Dolan on the radio asking me to make him an island. The thief's aftershave is nice, familiar. The sound of tools rattling from behind. My toe taps to the music.

You're OK, Mam, says the thief. I tell him to pull over immediately or I'll jump – I've done it before. He laughs but not in a conniving way. If he has the C word in him he hides it well. His eyes swell up and wet over when he stops laughing. There's great weight in the blanket he's put over my knees.

We'll tip home, Mam, he says. His voice lower. You've done your walk for today. And don't let on you went alone or I'll be the one that gets it.

My pension book slides across the dashboard as he slaps on the indicator and turns in at the head of the road. I wouldn't rule out the names Esther or Siobhan. He has a key to my front door, you'd nearly have to admire his thieving abilities. Liam runs up the hall when the door opens, a woman behind him. I wink at the dog to play along – I'll handle this mess.

How was town, Agnes? Oh the knees are mucky again. Liam don't tell me you let your mother walk in that rain! My mother will walk that road once a day as long as she's able, he says back, and we both know that won't be for much longer. What else has she got only her walk?

I could walk any of them under the table. I can make creamy porridge with just water and salt. The woman fusses about, wiping the muck off my tights and peeling the jacket off my back. Now she's hugging me and teary and kissing me on the cheek and whispering me to please be careful on them roads. Do you understand me, Agnes? This is what she asks me. Do I understand her. I say nothing. Rigid as stone. Cold stare. Because I understand everything and I know what she's after. I have the chequebook well hidden. I'll feed it to the dog before I give it to them. I eye my plants in the conservatory behind the kitchen. By the looks of it they haven't been messed with. The thief walks in behind me and goes to grab the Pedigree. I have to feed the dog, Mam. On your peril, I tell him.

The thief marches back out to the hallway and slams the front door shut. The woman jumps, still hanging out of me. She tells him he shouldn't be like that with his mother. He snorts and cocks the eyes and tears off into the kitchen like he owns the place.

The fairy comes flying down the stairs, all sorts hanging out of her. She pushes a coloured drawing into my hands. Nana, she says. Look! I finished it!

What I see is a picture of four people and a dog outside a house in the sun. Everyone's name on their T-shirts. Mammy, Daddy, Nana, Alice. *Alice.* I was right all along.

TO AVENGE A DEAD GLACIER

I

The woman in black silk and funeral veil unveils the plaque for Okjökull – *A letter to the future*. It's very light the way she lifts and folds up the thick velvet cloth, letting a small breeze move her face away from the rest of us. Miles and miles of Icelandic plains of brown and black and only the odd patch of white. I send a picture of the landscape to Bishop Ely. Then one of the plaque. *Thanks for talking me into travelling*, I tell him. *It all helps the cause*, he writes back. *God Bless*.

There must be a good hundred mourners up here, by their complexion mostly local. Some national media and a journalist from *The Guardian*. A group of Danish glaciologists gather away from the main crowd. They have them Volvo haircuts, loose bright-coloured trousers, voyager beards, all sorts of gadgets. A stray dog vibrates close to them, so much so it looks like she's feeling a class of cold that's hidden from the rest of us. The mouth is loose on her, the mange has the hair ate from around the nape and snout. Her tits are dry and swollen. She has the head of a lab, the arse of a collie. Behind her on the next ridge is a small cohort of men in uniform with binoculars. I sneak a picture of them and send it on to the Bishop.

An older woman moves close to the dog, sizes the animal up. She crouches and rubs its head. The dog takes to her and shakes a bit less. When the woman turns back towards the crowd, I see it's who I thought it was – Mary Robinson. The urge is to go over and say hello, of course, even though she doesn't know me. But I have her curls and long neck and fancy suits so well stored in my mind. I have the tone of her strong voice. They sang Simon & Garfunkel on the streets of Ballina the night she was inaugurated. My mother recorded the RTÉ news special and played it back every few weeks afterwards. *Heaven holds a place for those who pray*, she etched into a concrete border of a raised bed out the back of our house. I rubbed white vinegar and warm water into her fingertips afterwards. The words are still there to this day.

The woman in black silk walks over holding an unlit cigarette. Her eyes a Windolene blue. The elegant fingers on her like they've never been near smoke.

Lady, she says, that's that stray's name. I see her up here every time I visit Ok.

Have you been coming up here long?

Since I was a little girl I watched glaciers, she says. Ok in particular. It used to be nice days. Now it's more like visiting a hospice.

I wait for her to show some sign of humour but it doesn't come. She clicks at me with her thumb and I light her cigarette.

A young girl with cropped hair and Eskimo cheeks holds up a round placard encircled with a logo. The earth painted in bright greens and deep blues and two blobs of white at each of the poles: *Pull the Emergency Brake*. She glares at me like it's my fault.

Plates of *flatkaka* are passed around the wooden chapel. Cups of hot chocolate. There are no stained-glass windows or fancy paintings or even a tabernacle, but there's a look of polish off the pews. Fresh lilies on the altar. I take a picture for the Bishop. *Lutheran? Could well be*, he writes back, *not the worst sort.* I touch and smell the curtains of the confessional as I walk by. They've been dry-cleaned and pressed in the last week.

The glaciologists use the casket trolley to wheel their equipment and speakers up the aisle. My fingertips start to tremble when they squeak by my pew. I put the hands in the pockets and look at the woman in black silk, two rows up. She sits upright, facing straight ahead. She didn't bother with the hot chocolate. The chapel hisses with static.

A man stands between the speakers and introduces himself. An ex-priest turned activist. Physically himself and Bishop Ely are not far off each other. The small shrewd eyes, thin round glasses, receding silver crew cut, the square military jawbones. The ex-priest wears thick gold bands on each wrist. Some lines of sunlight bounce back off them.

I see grown men flying through the air to snatch at an O'Neills ball. Dr Hyde Park, Roscommon Town. My father and uncles around me. The Bishop bends down and tells me that's not a ball they're fighting over, it's solid gold, that's why they hold it so close to their chest. Mary Robinson would have been living in the Phoenix Park at the time.

Jack Charlton had given us a decent football team. The Bishop could already cover masses in the seminary in Maynooth and had no bother delivering a sermon if one of the priests was unavailable, even though he wasn't ordained yet himself.

He walked away at the end of that year before he took the vows. We had to house him for the Christmas while he recovered, my mother saying there was no way she'd leave her brother alone like that with no one to look after him. Something had opened up inside him one night in the chapel in Maynooth, is all he ever said about it. My father tutted his lips out the back a few days after the Bishop moved in with us. We were filling buckets of turf for the fuel box – I doing my best to keep time with him but the bog dust had closed my left eye and got up my nose and I fell behind.

They're all prone to the nervous breakdowns on that side of the family, he said without breaking his mechanical rhythm. Your mother'd be no different only for she met me.

I watched the Bishop leave for the Lebanon on Imbolc, 1 February, St Brigid's Day. *It's good luck to travel on the auspicious days of the calendar.* The first six months he spent volunteering in an orphanage close to Beirut. He's been on the road since.

A tight high-pitched scrunching sound comes through the speakers in the chapel. The feeling is like neurons in my brain being forced apart. I squint and shake the head to try right it. The ex-priest taps the mic very lightly, like he's checking it's on, but he keeps going, beating it like a very low drum. The movements and murmurs soon quieten down.

The short version of my talk today is that there is no talk. Or to be a little more precise, I do not have the words for my talk, because they do not exist. Not in my Icelandic or your English. Last week, I thought I was going to speak about those sounds we hear now. Those ticks and sucks and whistles coming from the speakers. I was going to compare them with dolphin talk, and then explain they were actually isolated sounds of melting glacial ice. I thought this would be clever. Like in my priest days, I would have used stories, not about crucifixions and resurrections, but about melting events, stack topples, calving, waterline sheet collapses, and together we would make sense of it all. But when the system itself collapses – when the ice shelf melts and does not get replenished – that old language becomes redundant. Because we do not yet have the word for the dark loss you sense, standing in the valley where Okjökull once stood. We lack the word for ocean currents that forget how to flow. Forget how to do their job. Like they have caught the memory disease from the old people who swim in their waters. And we have no word for the feeling us Icelandic people get as we watch our mountains float away with the sea. Maybe you can invent some new words for these events. Or better, maybe you can all stand up and actually do something, something that will stop all this from happening over and over.

The ex-priest steps back from the microphone and the glaciologists seem to turn up the volume. Pops and cracks and fractures that rattle the thin windows like we're being bombed. I sit on my hands to try still them. The woman in black has the head down. I should have sat beside her. She had glanced over at me when I was walking back down to my seat from the confessional but I looked away and kept going. I could have made small talk about dogs.

The sounds worsen. Pain-like groans. Choking and gurgling, bubbling. Eventually it settles back down to static. I take the hands out from under the legs and stretch the fingers. The ex-priest takes his seat off to the side and removes his rounded glasses. The hissy speakers are popped off. The quiet it leaves. People fidget in their seats again.

Just the once during a championship match did I bless myself – cemetery end of the main stand in the Hyde. A young corner forward from Boyle was after getting his arm broken and the bone jutted out through his skin. I sat quiet as my father and uncles roared abuse at the Galway fans, a tar-melting June bank-holiday weekend. My right hand shaking so much as I made a sign of the cross that someone jeered at my father, Is the young lad cold or what? He's like his mother, my uncle with the strong hare lip shouted back – He's afraid of his own shite. Bishop Ely turned and drew a punch on him. He drove his big fist up underneath the uncle's ribs. The sound and sight of my uncle trying to catch his breath, I suppose it was like an animal drowning in air.

The stray dog trembles outside the door of the chapel. I light up a rollie and she creeps over and nuzzles again my calf. Her shaking is contagious and little movements shoot up my leg. I can't understand how she's at it so much out here – there's no one to annoy her. Maybe she comes from a long line of dogs who've spent their lives watching glaciers die. She could be the one left with all those ice sounds trapped inside her. Now she's trying to shake them out once and for all. I put my hand on her and rub the thin muscle behind her ears.

It's the first time I've seen Lady that still, the woman in black silk says from behind me. I walk over and light another one of her cigarettes and we look over towards Okjökull.

What's your name?

Embla.

Nice name.

Thanks.

What's yours?

Shake.

What?

I got it in school and it stuck. Even the mother called me Shake in the end. Hey, did you know Ireland was once covered in ice?

I never been to Ireland.

There's an ancient woods between Roscommon and Athlone – St John's. A right off the N61 in Lecarrow. The toothwort and pipistrelle bats out there, they'd have roots back to those patches of ice.

Embla takes a sharp breath and grabs my arm. Her touch is light but it pulses up and down my body. I stare at her hand but she shakes me again. *Stari*, she says, pointing skywards with her smoking hand.

It would be impossible to put a number on the starlings, but they must be in their thousands. The murmuration moving in and out of itself over Okjökull. Bunching in close to form a solid black ball before groups of birds strip away into smaller diamond-shaped teams, teams that dip and orbit close to the ground in every direction, then coming back into a whole over our heads and shooting off south in an enormous arrow formation – like they've just picked up the glacier's scent. Embla leaves her hand on my arm a moment longer. I manage to get a picture of the starlings as they leave.

In my hotel room at night, I have the midnight sun and thin curtains. I have a million particles of dust suspended in the air over my head. I have no chance of sleep. A woman from Roscommon town with starlings on her feet is so vivid in my mind it's like she's going to open that small bathroom door any second. Her smile between shyness and confidence. Her high-cut fringe. Full white breasts. We used make love in her studio above her pub, the music from the DJ below rattling the jewellery box beside the bed. Emerald. Pearl. Sapphire. Amber. The DJ would play UB40, 'I Can't Help Falling in Love with You'. The Smiths, 'There Is a Light That Never Goes Out'. But the fucker would always finish up on Nine Inch Nails, 'Hurt'. It was like he could read the tea leaves. In the morning she'd bring me Lavazza coffee in bed and tell me there was no rush, no rush. Kissing my neck, the starlings swooping from her golden ankle bracelet down to her toes. She ran a mighty business and I knew I had a loving nest for the rest of my life if I wanted one. I left her on her birthday, no explanation. How I used turn my back on such gifts. How I didn't place my hand on Embla's today while I had the chance, instead of going for my phone.

II

Bossman comes looking for me in Frozen Foods. The clip-clop shoes on him, the hair gelled back, the small fat fingers. I have the door of the dessert freezer left ajar, examining the ice on the freezer wall. It leaves a nice numb feeling in my fingertips. It cools the mind.

How many fucking cigarette breaks have you had today and you only back from holidays?

He goes about herding me and my wheeled mop bucket towards a spillage on Aisle 3 – Wine, Beer and Spirits.

Why didn't you come immediately when I tannoyed you? If you want to be a professional space cadet, you can do it on your own watch. I knew you weren't worth a fuck when I took you on.

I stop and stretch to my full height and slam my mop to the floor, holding it straight up by my side. He turns back and taps his foot and looks up at me, biting his bottom lip. I could reach out and squash his little head like a grape. I could drive him through that 1 kilogram muesli display with a quick mop lunge to the chest. Until I fought one day in school without thinking, I never even knew I could fight.

A game of five-a-side in St Peter's gym and I headbutted the lad who'd hit Tadhg. I'd never practised headbutts but I set him on his arse and broke his nose and no one retaliated. Towering above every Leaving Cert in the school and I still only in Junior Cert.

In the yard toilets underneath the chaplain's house, I stood in front of the mirror and went about shaking the fight out of me. I cleaned the other boy's blood off my forehead. The mirror got a wipe down and I shined up the taps with water and soap and toilet paper. I got it as best I could then closed the eyes and let the rattle into every part of my body. Are you one of them fittin' spastics? a second year from the Batteries asked. His face swarmed with freckles and he sitting in a cubicle with the toilet seat down and smoking a Carrolls cigarette. He tapped the top of the twenty box in his shirt pocket – he'd rob them off his mother at night when she landed home drunk from Shine's Bar. I took next on his fag and smoked it down to a red horn.

Bossman hunkers and points to the spill from the Baileys display. His finger follows its flow as it seeps under the gondola rack and puddles out on Aisle 2 – Cereals and Grains. The incredulous look on his face as it touches off his high-heeled Mister shoe, you'd swear he never saw liquid spread before. I'll be losing an hour's pay for this. Maybe two. My fingertips start to buzz and my hands rattle, but I know by now how to put the brakes on when it's not the time. I erect the yellow Caution signs and steady the body and go at it. The movement brings firmness.

As a child I'd clean up for my mother after she taught her students to construct an edible balcony. Or showed them how to reuse tyres, how to plant a roof garden. The shears and loppers and hoes would need scrubbing. The splattered clay swept in from the edges of the rows. If I woke with the tremors, they'd be gone again by the time I'd hoovered the house and squeegeed the windows.

The world would be an impossible place without cleaners, Shake, she said when I landed my first cleaning job. Two weeks after failing the Leaving Cert. Imagine the mess we'd all be living in if it wasn't for the likes of you.

A young boy takes the corner fast and slips in the Baileys. Is he one of the Connaughtons? He has the long face of the Connaughtons. The fall takes nothing out of him. The way his father picks him up – he's not being brought up soft.

Does he play, he does? The young lad?

I have him out above with the Clann under-tens.

Midfield?

Not at all. He's mad for scores like the rest of them at that age.

He could be a great fielder of the ball yet. The big hands on him. If it's one thing the county needs.

No doubting that.

Bossman tells young Laura Cunnane on Till 1 that he's knocking off for an early lunch, he needs a run to clear the head, call him if there's any problems – his eyebrows raised in my direction. Laura Cunnane says nothing but smiles at him in a way gets a shake of the head from Maura Kilbride on the express checkout.

I have this notion. Maura Kilbride. I think she can see things happen long before they happen. She told me the length of time the last manager had left even before the woman got diagnosed. The change in her eyes. The crack in her voice. The colour of her unflushed piss in the broken staff toilet. And the shoplifters from town stay away every shift Maura works – it's like they know well that she knows well. In another time, Maura, she's the elder of the tribe. But here she is boxed in behind a SuperValu cash register.

If that was a thousand gallons of spilt oil below your mop and bucket, Maura whispered to me the first week I worked the aisles, they'd all walk around it to get to the deli counter. She smiled and laughed after she said it but her eyes didn't seem to find it that funny. Eyes that are always watery. The left lid drooping down much more than the right.

Yourself and the Bishop, Maura. Yee could be a great match for each other.

I have no need of a man. There's enough on my plate keeping tabs on the brother.

We take a selfie for the Bishop by the bakery but Maura sticks to her guns. She doesn't fix the hair or dust the dandruff from her shoulders. Without smiling she holds her small fist up in the air.

Solidarity is all I can offer that man, she says as I try squeeze the two of us into the frame.

When the Bishop doesn't respond to the photo, I send on a link to a HoganStand article on the Roscommon minors' championship game again Leitrim. I get the thumbs up five minutes later.

All work begins in the heart, my mother would say to her new permaculture students. She had a way of changing the sound of her voice when she spoke about the important things. She would slow her breathing, make eye contact with everyone around her. She could encase you with her statements.

The heart forms first in all species, she'd begin. Every other organ is derived from and induced by the heart. The heart sends more signals to the nervous system and the brain than the other way around, so all work must begin in the heart. Amen, I would say to myself, but I often caught some of her students looking up at her like there was something more than just a gardening class happening. There were days they usen't even take notes as my mother slowly read through the fundamentals of permaculture ecology. Care. Observe. Interact. Pay attention. Self-regulate. Respond to change. Envision. Intervene. Mimic the patterns of the natural world. Use edges. Value the marginal.

At the end of each weekend course, she'd tell them to sink their hands deep into the soil. Just leave them there for five minutes, everybody, would be her instruction. When our hands come into contact with the earth's soil, a bacteria called *mycobacterium vaccae* enters the body. It's nature's very own Prozac.

III

The back of Maura Kilbride's Nissan Micra is atrocious. Documents, rally posters, newspaper cutouts, flattened paper cups, ash. I have to sit on my hands to stop them cleaning. The Friday evening of a long weekend. Maura is up front on hunger strike, and judging by our supplies, so am I.

That house began life as a cottage – Maura leans into her steering wheel as she talks. Those slates were once golden thatch. A Derwin man built the extension out the back to make it T-shaped, and different outhouses cropped up over the years. The wonky fences are the brother's handiwork.

She stares at the tree stumps covered in sawdust. The chainsaw. Scene of the crime, she says to me in the rear-view mirror. But there's no way that ignoramus cuts down any more trees from our childhood, not as long as I'm set to starve myself.

Other back-seat visitors to her car have signed the ceiling. *Shell to Hell. Tara is Divinity. Heat up the dinner, not the planet. Free the Rossport 5.* A sketch of a devil with a red and yellow shell tattooed to his forehead. Oil spilling from his mouth. Gas from his ears. She passes me back a black marker. All the darkness above me makes the legs start to go. I tell her it's nothing, just some pent-up energy. I'll walk it off in a bit. *Rossies for the win*, I scribble between the devil and Tara.

Things slow down without food. The silence goes well with the rain. Her brother's big white head appears out the front door. The teapot held high in the air.

Around dusk he revs up the chainsaw. A steady line of smoke rises from the chimney. How long since you talked to the brother, Maura?

He rings me all the time, but things haven't been the same since they left him the place. They said I was too loose to look after it, and now look at it. As bald and miserable as himself. This place was like Eden when we were young. There wasn't a colour not visible in those fields and bushes and drains.

Do you want me to go talk to him, Maura? He looks fairly approachable.

Don't budge from that seat, Shake.

I won't so.

By the following morning the colour has faded more from her face. She's getting dizzy. I ask her would she not let me walk back into town – I'd feed her something on the sly and the brother wouldn't be any the wiser. But she just stares out the windscreen at the cottage, the stumps of ash and oak. The small window at the end where she slept as a girl. The look on her face no different than if she were waiting for traffic lights to change.

If he goes at that yew, she tells me – I can handle the rest of them, but the yew.

Let me talk to him, Maura.

Stay where you are.

Sunday at noon the brother walks from the house carrying a picnic basket. As he squeezes himself into the passenger seat I see he has Maura's humped nose. If he had hair he'd be a dead ringer. There isn't a pick on either of them. He smells of machine oil and animals and Old Spice. His cord trousers are clean but not pressed. Maura is forty hours into the fast. It feels like four hundred.

Will I get out, Maura?

It's him that'll be getting out.

Sound, Maura.

We're going to drink tea and ate sandwiches, ya daft aul bat.

Daft? I'm not the one cutting down the things I need to breathe fresh air.

There's plenty of them all the time around the place.

Are you going at the yew? I ask him. It's the yew she's really worried about. But he doesn't answer me. The picnic basket is flipped open and a cup lands on my lap. He places two more up on the dashboard and opens up a tinfoil parcel and places it behind the gearstick. He points between the brown and white sandwiches – beef and brown sauce, egg and onion. No one goes for them but we all want them. You'd know by the quiet.

This car could do with a clean, Maw, he says, as he pours tea for himself from his thermos. I'll do it for you if you like.

Maybe we should get the chainsaw at it, she says back.

I'll stop cutting if you ate a sandwich.

The damage is done already.

I told you on the phone, Maw, the two ashes had the dieback disease.

And the elder at Christmas? And the oak? And the rowans you took out last summer? Do you know what they'd do to you back in the day for cutting down the sacred trees?

You can't threaten to starve yourself every time I get the chainsaw out.

You were the same as a boy. Always hitting things and cutting and breaking. What's wrong with you all?

The brother goes silent and sups from his tea but leaves the cup up in front of his mouth. I can't decide if it's the egg and onion or the beef and brown sauce that has me like this. I'd ate that seat in front of me. I'm praying for Maura to let up the white smoke, but I'll hold as long as she holds.

I have nothing to do, Maw, he says eventually. I like to be at something.

There's no malice in the brother's eyes. The whites are watered like Maura's. Thin red veins cover his cheeks like roots. His hands are black with hair.

A +354 number flashes up on my screen and I jump out of the car like it's on fire. I don't believe it's her so I ask can we switch to video chat in case it's someone taking the piss. It's the first time I've seen her face without the veil. It takes me a minute to stop gaping and get the words going. She's beside the plaque on Okjökull and Lady is behind her – shaking like it's all just about to end. I tell Embla what I'm at. I let her see Maura and the brother in the Micra over my shoulder. I walk her around the yard, show her the outhouses. Explain how the roof used to look. I sit down at the trunk of the yew.

Come visit, I say without thinking.

No no, I can't travel, she says.

Why?

Why do you ask why? It's not right to fly, obviously, she says. The carbon.

Of course, of course, I let on.

Look, I have to go, she says. I'm going to try and take Lady for a walk away from here. Put some salt into Maura's water if she doesn't take any food. Otherwise she'll get the migraine.

OK, I will. Try and bring Lady home with you.

I will.

Maura has a cup of tea in her hand when I get back into the Micra. There are some crumbs on her lap. I grab two egg and onion sandwiches and bite through both at the same time. The brother turns around and fills my cup from his flask.

I have no sugar.

No bother.

And I have no biscuits neither.

Not a bother, I say, and I grab two beef and brown sauce.

There's no talk in the front but the feeling in the car is not a bad one. Maura looks settled again. The rain starts tapping the roof. The slow flap of the wipers. The three of us transfixed on the yew.

I'm sorry, Maw, he says, and pours the last of the flask into her cup.

I reach between the seats and turn on the radio just as the ball is being thrown in for the Connacht final. We'll listen to this, I tell them. I have a few pound on Roscommon.

IV

The night my mother passed away, I was heading the opposite direction. Burrowed down into a tunnel on the Hill of Tara. A chain from a brace around my neck to the shuttering above my head. The body in a constant tremble, but not the good sort.

I'd pushed my ear to the ground the day I landed at Rath Lugh. There was music rising up from the earth itself – I would have put money on it. A young man walked up through the trees with his top off. His skin the complexion of a tin of Pledge. He wore green combats. Black high-laced boots. An army helmet with *One Love* scrawled across the front and a gold spiral on a chain around his neck. In a beautiful London accent he told me his name was Alexander.

The camp has fractured, blood. Hardcore front-liners here on Rath Lugh. Spiritual hold-the-spacers over on the hill itself. Take your pick, but the destruction's already irreparable. Ancient forest groves felled and flattened for roundabout malarky. Road shapes being cut left, right and centre. Neolithic burial sites dug up with ancestral remains bagged and tagged, thank you very much. And the Lia Fáil? The old inauguration stone for the High King of Ireland? Who knows, blood. Probably be dug up some day and displayed inside a Tara Theme Park. Try and get some proper coin out of it.

He stopped to look around and scan the area. His voice lowered when I asked him about the plan of action.

From here on in, it's guerrilla tactics. Things need to get more militant. Men's circles and gong baths and fucking build-a-bender workshops are not going to turn this shit around.

Go on, Alexander, I said.

For a start, we've got the tunnel on the go. Jo Sax's gone and burrowed herself down there to stop the work happening on one of the last holdouts. It's worked well so far, blood, but more needs to be done.

What exactly needs to be done, Alexander? I'm here to participate.

Sssssh, blood. He hunkered and patted the ground with his fingers. Listen. She's playing her sax down there.

I put the hand up the following night to take a shift in the tunnel. Jo Sax had done four days and nights. A whole crew of people were on hand to get her out, but she pushed the sax out first. It was handled like a child. When they got her up, she had finger-strips of muck painted across both her cheeks. Her hair had natural dreads, an undercut running up the side. She wore a string vest with no bra. A white Hindu bindi stone on her forehead. It was like she was crawling out of a myth. I could think of nothing else on the way down only her string vest and bindi. The smell of Lavazza coffee in bed. Alexander watched me down the long vertical shaft until I let him know I was sound.

The tunnel itself was impressive. At the end a small chamber, angled in below the site under threat. All sides well shored with steel supports. The final piece of shoring covering the chamber was where Alexander told me I must lock-on. If they grab your feet and try take you out by force, the whole lot will come down. It's common practice on all the sites back home, blood. Effective. Inhibits. Distracts.

I couldn't stand up in the chamber but I could stand up in the shaft. There was a stash of dried and canned food and gallons of water. Enough nuts to feed a small army. Tonnes and tonnes of black earth inches above my head.

On the second night I got a chemical taste off the air. It hadn't rained but the earth seemed much damper than the day before. A smell like sheds. The body sagged and my mind couldn't hold a thought. I saw the home number come up on the phone but I couldn't answer. Talking didn't seem safe. It was like someone could hear my thoughts.

My mother's voice sounded from above. It was as sweet as I'd ever heard it. Younger. It wrapped itself around me like a shield of sound. She spoke of giving light, baking bread, the medicinal power of hawthorn and oak.

I'm OK, Mam, don't worry, I shouted up.

I thought it could be a flashback to my childhood. A flashback to the womb. I didn't know she was saying goodbye.

I stuck my index finger up between two lengths of shoring and smelt the soil. Roundup, that's the bastard smell I was getting. And Rentokil, maybe antifreeze. The security guards were trying to smoke me out. I messaged Alexander – *Get me the fuck up out of here. I'm done.*

I still get messages from him, Alexander, even though I never go to any of his call-outs. Out of them all, he was the only one who came to my mother's removal. He sang Joe Strummer, a cappella, in Shine's the night we buried her. Slow as a lullaby. He'd tweaked the lyrics to make it more about her. *Lord, there goes Lady Appleseed. She might pass by in our hour of need.*

V

Maura blows on a spoonful of canteen soup while checking the indie news sites on the Monday. A message pops in from Bishop Ely.

Where is he at it?

He says he's on the south coast of Spain, Maura. The ferry terminal in Algeciras.

On his tod?

He's standing between two women in a café. The photo is labelled *Sahrawi*.

Sah-rawi, Maura says back. Makes sense. Sounds like Sahara. What are they like?

They're wearing long red outfits, head to toe. *M'lahfas*.

Head to toe for the sun.

A sort of a deli red, I tell her.

And himself?

The Bishop has something similar on but all white. *Daraa.*

Good desert colour. But give me the till any day over the sand and that lunatic heat. There's probably more trees in my home place than there is in all that desert over there. What else does he say?

He says the white is for special occasions only, it's to mark his send-off. The women are the ones doing the fighting on the Western Saharan front, apparently, so he's going to leave them to it.

I'm off to Ukraine, Shake. I'm travelling with a comedian from home. She has a one-liner for every scenario imaginable. Even if the Black and Tans were to stop us, she'd have them in stitches before they got to cock their rifles.

Maura goes quiet. She tackles the soup again, studying it like she's trying to figure out what it is. I hope that comedian has a few Russian jokes up her sleeve, she says.

VI

A cassette arrives in the post. *Recent Events.* The Icelandic stamp on the envelope. A picture of the two of them in bed.

Not getting much sleep lately. When I do I dream bad, so we made you this tape. Love, Embla and Lady.

I spend ten minutes looking at the word *Love*. The word *Embla*. I think about nothing else. The body and mind still like rock. I root out the old Walkman in the attic and stick the cassette in. The ticks and whistles of the ice cool the head.

Put this sprig of lavender under the pillow at night. It'll help with the sleep and the dreams. If you end up in the land of the dead, don't worry, that's what's meant to happen – the mother was a herbalist. The lavender will bring you back safe and sound. And please come visit. I have the money here saved for your flights. We'll plant saplings together in St John's for the offset.

VII

I sit alone up the front of the Bus Éireann to Boyle, the driver bopping up and down in his seat. I want to ask him to either turn up or down that radio. All's to be heard is drone. I say nothing. When I see Tulsk on the horizon, I give him the tap on the shoulder.

Are you sure you know where you're going? he asks me as I step off at the crossroads.

I'm off to meet the devil himself, I tell him, with a nod back over the shoulder.

I have you now, he says.

Rathcroghan is dotted with sinkholes and mounds, remnants from the days of Queen Maeve. Walking down the boreen for Oweynagcat, I see someone out the corner of my eye. A farmer in mould-green overalls and a shock of dyed black hair. He walks away into a small barn. In the adjacent field is the hidden entrance, leading underground into the cave of the cats. The gates to hell, as the poets call it. I start to root around in my rucksack.

They're not going down there themselves at the minute, the farmer shouts over from outside the barn.

What's that?

The officials – if that's what you'd call them – what look after the place. They're staying away this past whileen.

Why are they staying away?

There's no air down in the cave – that's the party line anyways. They can't bring the tours down, is the thing, if there's no air. Do you get what I'm saying?

Right. What do you think yourself?

I think you can do anything these days but you can say nothing. So I'll say nothing.

Sound, I says.

I climb into the wet gear, and as I'm checking the batteries in my head torch, the farmer shouts back over.

That's the spirit, he says. Fuck them!

The air is heavy and cold, muck and rock underfoot. An ogham lintel close to the entrance – *Fraech, son of Medb*. There's no option but to hunker all the way in the blackness until the large souterrain opens up. Its long limestone cavern shaped like a cat with its feline spine up, ready to pounce. The breathing calms and the shoulders soften. I switch the head torch from white light to red and the top of the tunnel sparkles like the sky. The air thickens the further in I go so I leave longer between each breath. Every step sucks and squelches. A bit of a tremble moves up my back and my arms start to go. The legs vibrate. I stall and switch off the torch.

It's what the Kalahari Bushmen do, I told my father the first time he found me rattling in the back shed after he'd sent me out for a bucket of turf. Shaking is what all animals do when they've had a close call.

You've had no close call, ya fool – you've barely gone beyond the end of the road yet.

I have a book upstairs, I told him. The Kalahari say they do the shaking because it loosens things up inside them, all the stuff that's been stuck there for a while and is doing them no good. They say it leaves them lighter on their feet.

Look it, all you're going to loosen when you're at that shite is a few more screws up in that little head of yours. Now leave off with the voodoo talk or you'll end up like that godfather of yours in there. Hardly able to wipe his own arse and he meant to be some big-shot priest by now.

I brought in the turf and loaded it into the turf box. Looking around for my book, I noticed the father staring in at the stove. There was a load of paper crumpling up into a black ball in the flames. You may forget about that shaking business now, he said.

A trembling jolts into my left shoulder and runs across my neck and down my spine. I can no longer feel the cave floor beneath me. The whole trunk of my body is in a light spasm. Eyes open or closed, it doesn't matter – an image of my mother is up there at the top of the cave in the curve of the long thin valley. She is thumbing words into wet concrete. I lose my footing and slip back and bang my head.

The white specks of rock that held the glow for moments after the torch went out have faded. The blackness so dark it has solidified around me. The muck sucking me down no different to quicksand. There's that cackle of my harelipped uncle when he used hold my squeegee out of reach. My father laughing along.

I flick the torch on to full bright white and scramble back up the rocky tunnel. I slip again under the ogham lintel and two tourists with Canadian maple leaves on their hoodies drag me up out of the place. They don't seem to notice I'm head to toe in shite.

Hey there. How was it?

They don't call it the fucking gates to hell for nothing, I tell them.

Do you mind taking our picture in front of the entrance?

I don't.

Thank you.

No bother.

I make it a six-hour walk from the cave of the cats to Tarmonbarry. I stop at Tulsk and Lord Edwards GAA Club to have the sandwiches. Sitting in the small stand, the green of the pitch is like a tranquillizer. Small markings of kids' graffiti. Beaded love hearts. Smiley faces. A sign up beside the halfway line – *The players are children. The coaches are volunteers. The referees are human.*

The fresh cup of thermos tea steams my face. The tuna sandwiches always feel good for the head. I text Embla a picture of the sign.

On the way to Tarmonbarry.

What's Tarmonbarry?

Maura Kilbride told me there's a well beside the old church over there. She said the well has cures.

What's a cure?

Something that fixes people. Apparently the place is alive with rags tied to bushes.

Who ties rags to bushes?

The people looking for the cures, I suppose.

Take a picture of the rags.

OK.

Be careful.

I will.

Ask for a cure for Lady.

Good shout.

What?

Good idea.

In Tarmonbarry the white rags look like dead lilies in the moonlight. A decent blast of wind passes through and they move about and collapse again in the calm. I bivouac in the small woods close to the graveyard, the breeze cradling the hammock back and forth. I check the phone before sleep, like a fool.

Touring the war-hit provinces, Shake. We spent last night in Moshchun, a little village an hour outside Kiev. Two-thirds of the houses have been flattened. We put on a nice show in a makeshift bunker on the edge of the village. I gave a morning service, six in attendance, you have to start small. An elderly woman invited me home for food. The house looked normal from the front but we walked through to her kitchen and all I saw was green fields where her back wall should have been. Luckily enough the oven survived unscathed. We roasted potatoes she'd grown herself and baked hot-cross buns. Her name was Masha. She pointed out towards her vegetable patch as we waited for the buns to cook. It took me a while before I copped on she was really pointing at the rocket shell that blew half her house away. She had planted vegetables around it. She stuffed my rucksack with shallots before we left.

The following morning I rip a strip of cloth from my T-shirt and write out a note and tie it to the bush beside the well. I rip two more strips and write more notes. The statue of St Barry is decorated in rosary beads and prayer beads. St Francis of Assisi pendants. Mass cards. Someone has put a gold watch on his right wrist. There's a shattered Swatch on his left. Thin blue shoelaces tied around his walking staff. A bag of baby clothes at his feet. Loose change. The necklace of decorative paper flowers makes him look like a Buddhist deity.

I drink down some of the water from the well on the way out. It's the same sickness has us all, the Bishop reckons. Becoming aware of it doesn't rid you of it. I throw another drop into me before I leave.

VIII

The Bishop is kept up to date about everything. Embla and Lady moving over and us all living together in my parents' old home. Maura being made supervisor at work. Finding the copy of the Kalahari book in the attic that my father said he'd burnt – he'd placed it in a plastic sleeve first before storing it between two larger books. Alexander being tumbled out of his treehouse by private security guards on the HS2 sites in England. The native woodland that was felled the next day. *Shiva give and Shiva take, blood. But the show goes on.* Embla and myself trying to have a baby. It could be my end, I tell him, the problem. Embla is very tuned into her body. When she ovulates, she can smell the meadowsweet from the field to the rear of our house, as if it were growing all over our bedroom carpet.

I'm sorry I haven't written in so long, Shake. I'm supposing you know where I am. I came across the kids on my second day here. I found them rummaging for food in the rubble where their house used to be. I'm wearing a ring and cassock and biretta that I picked up in Ukraine. These soldiers need to see what they're dealing with. Does my time served in the seminary grant me this one pass to wear the robes? You'd need some sort of a shield in this place is all I know.

The good news is we're actually only a few hours' walk from the border. It's just that my little companions, they like to travel at a slowish rate. And what with the energy levels and the heat, it'll take us a few days to get there. The plan is to walk straight up to the checkpoint and march these children out of here. I see no other way of keeping them alive. The last thing they ate was a stray cat. They spent a morning chasing it down in the street. I helped them cook it. Photo attached (of us, not the cat). God bless.

He's pushing a makeshift wheelbarrow through a street which is mostly debris. One wall remains untouched, its window still closed, with nothing behind it only more wreckage. It's difficult to say what the area was in the past.

One of the children sits high up on the wheelbarrow and smiles at the camera. Some strands of hair look glued to her cheek, the rest like she's plugged into something. Her face a pasty grey. The other three look ahead as if they're trying to remember the way. It's the first time I've seen Ely dressed up as a bishop. But the garments are filthy – a manual scrub before a 90-degree spin cycle at least, I tell Embla. The white tippet will need a deep bleach, if it's to be salvaged at all. You could forget about the shoes. His face is as gaunt as the children's. He must have lost the glasses. There's a line of sand-coloured army tanks on an embankment a few hundred yards behind them.

I think he just needs to come home now, I tell her. He just needs to settle a bit for once. He can't keep trying to fix it all. He says he's bringing them children with him. How in the name of God is he going to pull this one off? But what if he makes it? We could adopt them, could we not?

Embla tries to get the phone off me. Lady backs into a corner and growls and I've never heard her like that before. As I study the dog, Embla pries the phone out of my hands.

Sleep, she tells me. Just try to sleep. Pretty much all the weekend you are looking at that phone.

Leave the lamp on all night, I tell her. Light whatever candles we have.

She stays awake until dawn just to hold my head in her arms.

There's a great smell of lavender off the pillow in the morning. Lady noses the door open and walks over and rattles by the side of the bed. I tap the mattress and she jumps up. The mange has cleared up nicely. She's starting to put on weight.

I have to go to work soon, Embla.

And you can go?

I'm fine.

Maybe go early and get wild garlic for soup?

OK.

And one of the apple cakes from work.

Apple tarts, I say. No bother.

Down the bridle path I rip a small bit of leaf off a head of wild garlic and stick it under the tongue. The leaf should smell no different to the clove once it's ready. I cut off two big bunches midway down the stem and tie them off and put them in the backpack. The smell of garlic off my fingers. The smell of Embla. Of Lady. When she ovulates, Embla, she lets me in behind her as soon as I wake, knowing I'll come harder and faster. When I finish, she quickly rolls over onto her back and pulls her knees up to her chest. I lie with her and help hold her knees up and we both briefly picture what might be happening inside. But they say once a year has passed at that stuff, there's probably something amiss.

If he makes it out of there, I said this morning, but I didn't even have to finish my sentence. She was already nodding her head in agreement.

We take the four of them, no problem, she said.

I took out the phone and looked at the picture again. I hadn't even noticed the big heart drawn onto the smiling girl's T-shirt until Embla showed me. She sitting like a princess in the wheelbarrow. Embla pointed to a mole on her cheek, and the small distance between her nose and upper lip. The texture of her hair. The same traits in the other children.

Siblings, I said.

What?

They're brothers and sister.

Yes yes.

They'll have to stay together, Embla.

One way or other, she said, we should adopt some children that really need us. That way we getting back at the world.

It was the way she said one way or other – I knew she thought they wouldn't make it. But I was already imagining what the names of those children were, what second names we could give them. How we'd all live together here, the smiling girl our unspoken favourite, but I couldn't look at the photo again without seeing the tanks.

The tingling starts in my fingertips and thighs in the cleaning press before I even get the uniform on me at work. My head vibrates like I've bitten down on a high-voltage cable. Bossman storms in.

You're fucking late again!

When I turn around he looks muddled. He comes a bit closer.

Are you alright? Have you taken something?

My calves and hips and pelvis start to go and I can't put the brakes on. It's in the chest and shoulders and neck and arms. Bossman looks frozen – I reach out to hold onto him. He steps closer again.

Jesus, it's OK, son. What happened?

He puts his hand on my shoulders but the trembling often becomes intenser when the circuit is closed. It scrubs through my head like a brush. Even my eyes spasm and the bottles of bleach and rolls of blue paper and wipes and overalls all seem to be tremoring along with me.

I come to on the floor with himself and Maura Kilbride standing over me. Maura helps me up and walks me to the canteen.

I haven't eaten proper all weekend, Maura. That might be it.

The tea she makes is way too sweet but she sits across from me and encourages me to drink it anyways. I reach out and touch the back of her long wrinkled hand. I rub the creases on her skin. Her hands almost fully blue with veins.

Come over for dinner, Maura. I want you to meet Embla and Lady. And the Bishop will be there soon.

Once there's no funny business, she says back.

He's bringing some new friends. We're going to make some changes around the place.

She says nothing. Just nudges the cup closer to me and pours more tea.

Young Laura Cunnane walks in and sits across from us. She watches mine and Maura's hands and her eyes are close to falling out of her head. She looks to Bossman like he should do something, but he just nods in a light way towards the door and talks lower than usual.

Maura's till needs covering, Laura. And tell Joanne she's on cleaning for the rest of the day.

Laura Cunnane walks out and Bossman brings Maura and myself down a round of tea and toast. He tells Maura the plumber has been and the jacks are sorted.

Take your time, he says. I'm off for a run. He gives me a wink. And you should go home and rest.

I tell him thanks but I'm better when I'm working.

Fair play to you, he says.

IX

I write letters to Mary Robinson. To TDs. To ambassadors. NGOs. I spread missing-person posters online – cropping the picture of Bishop Ely and the children to remove the tanks.

We spend our free days pulling weeds and putting down Records and spring onions. Tea roses and geraniums and long-headed poppies. Rosemary and thyme. We plant my mother's favourite, trumpet lilies. We stick them down all over but none of them flower. We plan a trip to Seed Savers to get some advice.

On Sundays I dust out the dirt and clay and leaves from the mother's thumbed words in the concrete. Some mould has grown in the etchings of the letters. After a good power hose, I treat the mortar with an acrylic sealer.

We print and frame a large copy of the wheelbarrow picture for the centre of the mantelpiece. The one of him and the Sahrawi women beside it. The one of myself and the Bishop outside the Hyde, day of the Connacht Final. 1994. Roscommon 0–13: Mayo 1–9, after a replay.

I check my emails every hour. The phone rarely rings. People online contact me looking for news. Everyone is supportive, sympathetic. Mary Robinson wishes there was something she could do.

There are white rags flapping in Tarmonbarry. There is special-offer bunting hanging over the deli counter in work. I mop towards it, carrying it all with me like alms.

MOTHER VS DEEP BLUE

OPENING

Rudolf Spielmann said the beauty of a game of chess can only be assessed by the sacrifices it contains (*The Art of the Sacrifice*, 1935). Mother read Spielmann as a child. She played club chess through national school and earned the title of FIDE Master in 1978. Whenever I asked her about giving up competitive chess, she spoke of her parents. They pushed her too hard. The pressure ruined her love for the game.

Mother began teaching me chess at a very young age. It'll help you make better decisions, she would say. It will make you more creative. But no tournaments, no FIDE ranking events. Just play and you'll always have it.

Around the same time she converted the spare bedroom into a small studio. I helped her to rip up skirting boards and dump old furniture. All that was left was her easel in the centre. A side desk with paints. A chess board on a small coffee table in the corner, two mini stools either side, and her old copy of Rudolf Spielmann on the window sill. She was rediscovering the joy of the game, not in the playing of it, but in the painting of it. I watched her every evening after school.

Things started off very simple. Main lines from classic bouts were drawn and layers of colour were superimposed for the emotions that arise during games. White for the waiting move, the passive play. Blue for calm intellect. Purple for the psychology, the mind trickery. Red for sacrifice. Black for the paranoia. Her muse from the start was Kasparov.

It was the aesthetic of how Kasparov went about his business that really moved Mother. The iconic head-holding pose as he tried to vice-grip the right move from his mind. The patterns that appeared on his side of the board to signal what was coming. The Sicilian Najdorf. The Scotch Game. The Grünfeld (Exchange Variation). The Petrov Defence. And what Kasparov sought and what Mother wanted to capture was the unique positional pattern a brilliancy could make. A thing brand new put on display upon its conception, so beautiful and destructive that it could end games on the spot. Inflict psychological damage. End careers. Crown Kasparov, the Beast from Baku, as world champion.

Two days after my sixteenth birthday the news came in that Kasparov had won his first match against IBM's Deep Blue. The only surprise was that he didn't win by more. Mother was already sketching out lines from the penultimate game when I arrived home. But I remember her voice not sounding right, like she was afraid she would wake someone even though it was just the two of us in the house. The way she didn't turn to me when she spoke like she normally did.

Art must always make a connection, son.

Connection, I said. Cool.

Within art there has to be something for people to feel. To recognize.

OK.

I tell my canvases everything – you know that, don't you? That's the sacrifice we make. A true artist can leave nothing out.

I didn't respond. She had lost me by this stage.

The work Mother did on Kasparov brought her success enough that she could leave her accountancy job and focus solely on the art. Through the guts of the nineties, she created abstract landscapes and Kasparov's sharp lines provided the cartographic nodes. Her boarded worlds always rose up in the centre, showing the importance of these squares. Showing the constant power struggle between two people.

Her triptych on the first world championship match between Kasparov and Karpov (Moscow, 1985) was the work that got her shortlisted for the Turner Prize. Game 16 from that match went down as one of Kasparov's immortals. With the black pieces he managed to outpost a heavily protected knight deep into Karpovian territory. An earlier pawn sacrifice allowed him to do this, a carbon copy of a move he had attempted in Game 12. Karpov accepted the poisoned sacrifice, advanced his C and E pawns, and was left with no protectors to kick away the knight which now controlled the board. For the following eighteen moves, this knight controlled the whole world of chess. Its domination kept white's rooks out of the game and left one of Karpov's own knights stranded out in no man's land on A4.

That is what a brilliancy is, Mother explained to me as she stood back and tilted her head up at the giant snapshot of the game postered to her studio wall. That is complete intellectual strangulation – and I could not tell if she was happy or sad as she spoke.

By the time Kasparov played knight to D3 in Moscow (Game 16, Move 16), Karpov was already in zugzwang – a nightmare situation where, even though it is your turn, any move is detrimental to your position. By Move 34, Karpov was forced to sacrifice his queen just to remove the knight, but it came too late. Kasparov took the title from him and became the youngest-ever world champion at just twenty-two years old. He would remain so for fifteen years and would retain his world-number-one status for the rest of his professional career. At his peak, the Beast from Baku was on the level of all previous chess gods. He was Bobby Fischer. Mikhail Tal. Capablanca. Mother's interpretation of his immortal in Moscow was entitled *Octopus Knight*.

I remember Mother spending full days watching top-ranking chess players simultaneously compose and perform their work while she lined and coloured their moves. She figured out ways to snare Kasparov's sharp lines, his deviations, his traps. She captured his opponent's paranoia, and even Kasparov's own as he saw a weakness in one of his moves and left the board immediately after playing it, so as to distance his fear from his opponents, lest they seize on it. She painted players chasing ghosts, running from ghosts, as the paranoia in a game is sometimes enough to see threats that do not exist. And Kasparov, he could play the ghost move, the psychological move, then sit back and stare his opponent down as if he himself were haunting them. For a piece entitled *Death by Bishop* (oil on canvas, 72 x 56), Mother slashed her canvas with a thousand diagonals from bottom right to top left, just as Kasparov had run a thousand fianchettoed bishops along the diagonal from G2 to B7. Exposing fatal attacks. Leaving his opponent's pieces hanging.

The Guardian's art critic, Gillian Small, said in her review of the 1989 Turner Prize shortlist that Mother had captured Kasparov's thought processes and transposed them onto canvas. Small went on to detail how this took place. How Mother traced Kasparov's moves but left a time-trail echoing out behind to show each piece's complete path throughout a game. Each sequence of moves layered upon the next and showing the incredible sharp openings, the pawn pushes, the marshalling rooks, and ending on the positional masterpieces that Kasparov dedicated his life to finding. By the end of a game, by the end of a painting, what emerged on Mother's canvas was not some abstract mess that needed imagination and red wine to interpret, but real patterns of geometric beauty. This artist, said Small in her article, has managed to map the footprints of a mind. She has taken a snapshot of the subconscious to show what true creative genius looks like and laid it out for all to see on a 64 x 64 canvas.

The only problem for Mother and me was that my father did not take to her new lifestyle, to her new-found fame. It is the important work, she would say in her defence at the dinner table – the few times he would actually show up on time to eat with us – but he took nothing she said on board. For months he just attacked her decision to leave the stability of her nine to five, and my father was well able to play on the offensive, in more ways than one. He chewed his food in a circular way like cows do, with his mouth open. The sound of the food being masticated was amplified around the table. He knew it made me wince. Another favourite move of his was to look around the room after he spoke, sipping his expensive wine as he did so, like there were an adoring audience listening to him.

His smile would always strengthen when he felt he was starting to wear Mother's position down. Whatever line of defence she tried, it would fail. The swiftness of his responses, as much as what he said, made her words seem empty. It was this speed and ruthlessness that won him every single dinner-table battle.

Money's the only true language in this world, he would tell her as the exchanges came to a head. And who's going to fund little Ziggy Marley here when he's bigger and bolder?

But even when he talked about me, even when you could tell by his eyes he was getting worked up, he would never shout. He was too clever for that. His style was just to blitz out the sly comments.

Look, you're no Picasso, darlin', you're an accountant – an accounting technician before you met me, I might add.

He would never clear his plate away after he ate. He never thanked Mother for the food.

I will bring in my share still, Mother reassured me after the bigger of the arguments. The art was starting to pay off well, she explained. She'd always make enough to support us both.

MIDDLEGAME

In the run up to Kasparov's rematch with Deep Blue in New York, the idea touted at the time was 'The Brain's Last Stand' (*Newsweek*, 3 May 1997). Mother and myself, however, were not worried about the outcome. Kasparov had played computers before. He'd played Deep Blue's forefather, Deep Thought, in 1989 (Deep Thought 0: Kasparov 2). In 1996 he took Deep Blue out in their initial match behind closed doors, and so the rematch in New York had an exhibition feel to it, where the quirky celebrity challenger would eventually go down before the bout was over. The Beast from Baku wouldn't even have to go through all the gears to get the win – he was playing a mindless computer made of silicon and cables, not a fellow 2800 super-grandmaster.

Mother and myself booked into a fancy hotel for the rematch in New York. It was our first holiday alone together. We queued early outside the hall each day and wore matching *the brain will not be bested* T-shirts. A giant board with notated moves was projected onto a screen over the stage, and after each game, Kasparov and the IBM team would come out and face the crowd and take media questions. Kasparov dominated Game 1, but in Game 2, Deep Blue forced his resignation.

Up until that point in our chess lives, Mother would always explain to me that the chess-playing style of a computer was brute force. It was a slow-moving wall that closes in on its opponents and takes takes takes, capturing all available material regardless of outcome. A computer does not understand sacrifice, she would say, and it is blind to the dangers of accepting one. A computer lacks hunch and instinct, and it can never play a psychological move. And Kasparov, he had prepared to play a computer. He was battle hardened for the brute force, but in Game 2 towards the latter half of the middle game, he offered up some material, convinced the computer would take it, which would allow holes to be punctured in Deep Blue's defence. But Deep Blue did not do what a computer is supposed to do. It thought hard. It crashed. It rebooted. Kasparov sweated and paced and held his head in the corner of the stage as after the third reboot, with fresh buffers and logs to think through, Deep Blue refused the sacrificial pawn, a sacrifice in itself, and it played instead a beautiful move. It played a human move.

By Game 4 the bookies' odds began to swing. Spectators were quiet, sitting up straighter in their seats, small chess boards were out and lines were being analyzed and calculated. A Latino guy with micro-dreads and an FC Barça T-shirt in front of us left his seat every hour and came back with glazed eyes. I followed him out once and nodded at his hand and he smiled.

I don't know about you, he said to me, but that Deep Blue dude, that thing is playing some grandmaster shit.

Kasparov will hold, I told him. There's no way a computer beats the Beast.

He shook his head and laughed and left me to finish off the blunt.

And Kasparov did hold. We met him with a standing ovation as he walked across the stage after the penultimate game, having earned a third successive draw in a row, but the penny was starting to drop for all in attendance. We were no longer just cheering Kasparov on, we were cheering on ourselves. We were cheering on our biological brains and beating hearts and creative thinking minds.

Mother squeezed my hand through all the remaining tense periods of play, looking at me each time Kasparov found a way to protect himself, whispering in my ear, We have it, son, we have it. He is going to find a brilliancy and win the match. Just watch. And I did. I watched the match. I watched Kasparov. I watched the guy in the Barça jersey and I watched Mother. But her face was different to everybody else's. It was like she was watching an actual war as opposed to a gamified one.

At the end of Game 6, after Kasparov put out his hand in resignation, Mother's hand went limp in mine. She stared hard at the back of the seat in front of her. Kasparov himself went into a twelve-month period of grief after the match. He would eventually emerge and publicly state that he was not just defeated by Deep Blue in New York that day, he was killed.

When answering questions about Deep Blue's preparations, the IBM engineers played down speculation that it was prepared specifically to play Kasparov. Deep Blue did not know it was playing Kasparov, they stated. Deep Blue did not even know it was playing chess. But Mother would argue, Kasparov would argue, by Game 2, Move 36, Deep Blue knew exactly what it was doing.

On our flight home from New York, I tried coaxing Mother into playing a game of blitz on my travel board, but she turned away, staring out the porthole. Our game is dead, she said. She stopped painting in the latter half of that year. She returned to her job and her unused canvases were stored in the attic.

INTERMEZZO

The Mechanical Turk (Wolfgang von Kempelen, 1770) was a chess-playing apparatus that travelled the world in the eighteenth century. It won not all but the vast majority of its games. It was an automaton. A carnivalesque wooden box with a mechanical man making moves. The man's head and torso were visible above a wooden compartment that housed its apparatus. He wore the clothes of a sorcerer, and like a player deep in thought, his eyes roamed slow about the board.

Thousands gathered to watch the Mechanical Turk perform in exhibitions. It was labelled by some as witchcraft. As demonic. As Godly. Karl Gottlieb von Windisch wrote at the time about an old lady who had seen the machine in action and ran home to hide herself in a window seat. She said she was trying to distance herself from the evil spirit that possessed it (*Inanimate Reason*, 1784). But others were drawn to the Turk just to see what these new machines could do. What human functions they might replace in the future.

The Turk travelled the world during its eighty-four-year career. It beat grandmasters and royalty. Benjamin Franklin put up a good fight but fell apart in the endgame. Napoleon Bonaparte got smashed in less than twenty moves. In another game, Napoleon wrapped a shawl around the Turk's head and torso, but still went on to lose heavily. So I have to think to myself – did Napoleon feel in 1802 what Kasparov felt in New York in 1997? Was he paranoid? Did he suspect something was amiss or did he truly believe that a machine was this good at chess?

The writer Edgar Allan Poe debunked the Mechanical Turk in a famous essay ('Maelzel's Chess Player', 1836). Poe made the solid argument for a real grandmaster to be hidden inside making all the moves. If this were a pure chess-playing machine, it would never lose a single game. The fact that it lost meant there must be a human involved – there must be a *mind* operating the machine.

After analysing his rematch with Deep Blue, Kasparov started to think along the same lines. Perhaps he had read Poe's essay, or maybe someone had told him about the old woman hiding in the window seat, but one way or another, the paranoia took hold. There was something small and powerful hidden inside Deep Blue pulling all the levers. He demanded access to the data server room to inspect the server rack. The IBM engineers said, Read the small print, Garry, the data room is out of bounds. Kasparov then asked for a printout of Deep Blue's logs. Why all the crashes? Why the restarts? Why the great move after such a restart in Game 2? Read the small print, Garry. But what Kasparov truly wanted was to smash Deep Blue's titanium skull open and walk in and look around with his flashlight and grandmaster-detector device.

I wanted to do something similar to my father when he left us. I wanted to smash his head in and have a good look around inside. Find the ghost pulling the levers that controlled his hands to pack his suitcase and powered his legs to walk out the door. Find the mechanical voice box that made him say those words to Mother as he did so. But I began to overanalyse. I reviewed the last few years he'd lived with us, line by line. I wanted to find the blunders – the bad moves which caused all this. If we had picked apart his strategy and foresaw what he was at, we could have ended it all long ago. We could have wiped him clean off the board and started afresh, and perhaps Mother would never have left her art.

The white for passive play, the waiting move, that's him not coming home for dinner, I said to Mother once over the kitchen table. Is it not?

No. Not consciously, son. I have always said that I told my canvases everything when I painted, but that's not the way it works. I never set out to express anything in particular – I just followed the flow as it came.

But you knew at the time he was fucking about, did you not?

I had an idea, yes. And nice language, by the way. You were brought up well.

And that would have come out in the work, would it not?

It all came out, I suppose, yes.

Then why be so cryptic with me? You could have said that was what you were thinking all along. I could have done something.

Listen, you were a child back then, and by the looks of it you still are – you're just a drunk and stoned twenty-year-old child now. It wasn't easy leaving that world behind, you know, but when he left I couldn't go back. I couldn't paint. You had to be looked after.

Purple for the psychological move, I can see that now. Him telling you you were driving him away with your obsession with art and chess. I heard him say that. That you were never there for him. Purple equals his mind trickery, does it not? That oak set you bought me the Christmas before New York, it was that bastard who hid the white queen before I got up. Joking that you had bought a second-hand set. And it was the last Christmas he spent with us. It's his mind fuckery that's causing this very argument now.

Calm down, son. We're not arguing.

Red for sacrifice. Him sacrificing his family for his young accounting protégée. A very human move I feel. A pattern even. Did he not label you as his protégée before you married him? Did you not tell me that as a child? A nasty move, I said.

ENDGAME

I flew Mother to Washington last year to visit the National Museum of American History. Mother's senility meant she did not quiz me too much on why the big trip or why that museum. We landed at midday and were in the museum by 2 p.m. I led her downstairs to the technology exhibition and I walked her over to the corner display.

We stood in front of Deep Blue twenty-five years after it took out Kasparov. Twenty-four years after my father left us. Three years after Mother's senility had begun. Mother pushed her head again its titanium casing and I did not try to stop her. Her short-term memory was fading but she did not need an explanation as to what she was looking at. Touching the sign that told her it could calculate 200 million positions per second. Kasparov? Maybe two. She knew it was the same Deep Blue who could see hundreds of moves ahead at all times. Kasparov? Thirty. Max. And only at the beginning of a game when he was entering into a well-trodden and prepped main line. After that, once middle game was reached, Kasparov could see even fewer moves in front of him. In the endgame the same, unless it was a set mating net – a trap you cannot escape.

Mother pushed hard against Deep Blue. Against its 1.5 tonnes. Against its mind so large as to have been split between twin titanium 6 foot 5 cabinets. Its left and right lobes. Kasparov? 5 foot 9. Twelve stone. A 1.3 kilogram brain. Blood and bone he was, but mostly water.

How had he any hope against that monster, Mother? But she stayed leaning in against the machine, saying nothing.

I looked at her as we walked back upstairs. Her tears still enrage me. All the other art she could have produced over the last number of years if Deep Blue had not taken out her muse. If he had not left. If the IBM engineers had just tackled some other project and left our game alone. I wished for the courage to go back downstairs and call out Deep Blue. I wished for a mind imbued with enough processing power for 201 million positional moves a second. For the ability to see 500 moves into the future.

I waited close by as Mother used the bathroom. I sat on a beanbag and took out my phone and played a game of bullet chess. Then another. By the time I was three up I came out of the game and still no sign of her.

Each time she goes missing I fear the worst, even just around our house. It is only the two of us, and so if I go and do our weekly shop and come back and she is nowhere to be seen, my mind races. She has walked out onto the road. She has slipped out the back and cannot get up. She is alone somewhere, confused and scared.

I found a female security guard on her rounds and asked her to go into the toilet to check on Mother. The security guard reappeared – there was no one in there. She alerted her colleagues – Do not let a woman of this description leave the building. We searched the floor we were on – nothing. The security guard asked where we had spent most of our time and we made our way to the stairs. Halfway down, we met two male security guards helping her up the stairs – Mother had plugged out Deep Blue.

The security people fussed over Mother like she could collapse any minute. Mam, are you sure you're OK? Would you like some water? You are in a museum, do you know that, Mam? And as they ushered us towards the museum café, I realized, looking at them and listening to their words, that they thought her act a mistake. They felt sorry for her. They thought she thought she was plugging out her television set before going upstairs to bed. They did not recognize it for what it was. An act of sabotage. A beautiful move.

Our flight home was delayed so we played chess in the departure lounge on my travel board. Mother can still play well. Every time she looks at the board she sees a brand new game, but the lines and positions from a thousand grandmaster clashes are embedded within her. We drank more tea. Mother played black and laid out a solid Sicilian (Dragon Variation). By Move 15 she had me in a chess headlock.

I looked out the window at the runways and lines of people coming and going and little tractors taxiing enormous planes to and from their docks. Mother began sketching on our napkins. Kasparov and Deep Blue chatting on a bench in Central Park. Deep Blue holding its arms up and Kasparov running a stethoscope over its chest, shaking his head. Deep Blue leaning in and resting on Kasparov's shoulder. The Beast from Baku looking off into the distance, smiling to himself.

Your move, she said.

HUSH MAVOURNEEN, THE POLICE ARE WATCHING

I

By the canal there are large stretches of the purple flower, like the one does grow on the bog. The grass under the feet so dry it feels brittle. In fairness, the RTÉ woman did promise record high temperatures, and for once she's come good. That sort of light – Bry's voice clear as day in his mind – it'll fade the work. But Gerald pulls the top off anyways. His body needs the heat. It's cold work being around illness.

He looks down at his arms, he touches his face. The best thing about getting it done at first was that most people didn't recognize him. He used even have nightmares about losing it. Walking down Northgate Street like the invisible man, then a shower of rain would come and wash all the ink away.

The four girls who've been making their way up the far side of the canal are now directly across from him. Two of them in miniskirts and their full white thighs reflect the sun. Another in combats and a belly top has some script inked up her side. From here he's saying it's something exotic, Sanskrit, maybe. The fourth girl has the *Unknown Pleasures* T-shirt. Her hands are clawed under a king-size skin, rolling as she walks. The two skirted girls pull down on their hems as they pass opposite him, but the Sanskrit girl, she waves over and smiles.

He held another boy's hand crossing the weir wall in the late nineties. Fourteen years old but he'd already known for half that time. He would never see other boys together though, not like that, not in the town or on the television, so he quietened himself to the thoughts. Maybe that day on the weir it was the heat that loosened him up. It does give him the horn still. A day just like today, the earth hard. The Shannon low enough so you could walk the top of the wall, but a slip was still possible. Older boys with dogs and sleeve tattoos had their tops off in Burgess Park and drank flagons of cider and listened to acid techno. The kick drum wobbled across the water. The other boy's hand was bigger than his, easy to grip, like a very light grade of sandpaper. The boy's hair was speckled white and he smelt of lime and mastic. I've spent the summer attending my uncle on the sites, he explained to Gerald over the shoulder, halfway across. They held hands a few moments longer after they reached land but the techno boys farther up started to jeer at them and the other boy left. Gerald closed his hand in on itself and watched him walk away.

The Sanskrit girl and her friend are up behind him before he has a chance to put his top back on. Katie, the Sanskrit girl says without putting the hand out. And this is Bangle. He puts the head down. There are tiny globes of sweat on his black full arm sleeve. No design. No symbol. Just black ink from wrist to shoulder. Both sides. The girls stay a few paces away and the one in the Joy Division T-shirt sparks up. It looks too big for her hand. It's a blunt, the thinness, the pure smell – impressive for a pair of young ones to be smoking pure plant. The Sanskrit girl eyes his face and chest and asks what the thing running up around his body is. It's a vine so it is. Ah right. She checks out the black and red bramble bush circling his Adam's apple and asks, Are they big man hands keeping the bush open? They are. Cool. Where did you have all the work done? Bry Lavin. I've heard of him. Yeh, we have his family's cottage up the way. He's a bit under the weather at the minute but he's going to get better so he is.

The Sanskrit girl takes two quick hits and hands it to Bangle. My mother was a Bangles fan, she tells him. She couldn't decide which one she liked the most. Great name, he says. I always wonder why everyone has the same boring names. Bangle's great. Have you one yourself? I do. My name is Gerald.

The penny dropped during the first session in Bry's parlour close to the Light House Cinema, Smithfield – they were from the same town, different sides. Bry a good few years older and had left for Dublin before doing the Leaving Cert. Gerald had heard over and over since moving up himself that Bry Lavin was the man to go to. Bry didn't try talk him out of the full face he'd planned like all the other artists had. He'd ruin himself, they said. Full coverage wise, the face is a no-go area. He'd never get another job as long as he lived. But Bry loved the M.C. Escher idea for the right cheek. He tweaked it so that the river in the design ran down Gerald's nose. The large white birds that came up out of the checkerboard landscape, they crossed this river and become the starlings on his left cheek. Bry tinkered around with the murmuration of starlings until some flew north and got ever smaller until they disappeared into Gerald's low thick hairline. A few stray birds flew south and dove head-on into his black sleeve. Why starlings? I don't know. I think they have me brainwashed with the sky shows they do be doing.

During the third session the chat was on Count John McCormack. Gerald said he'd never really heard the Count in action, so Bry said they'd take a break to rectify the situation.

The feeling when the needle punched in and out, that intense electrical pain, it gave way to a throbbing relief once Bry lifted the needle away. The face buzzed with change. The want for more of the same pain shortly afterwards.

When he came out of the toilet he checked out Bry's portfolio on the coffee table. The photos of tribal art on the walls. A massive framed picture – *tā moko* – of a Samoan woman with her tongue pushed fully out and geometric leaves on her cheeks. Beside her – *moto* – a Māori man with lines spiralling out from his nose.

A crackly sound came through the speakers and Bry walked over to him with two coffees. It's called 'Una Furtiva Lagrima'. *A furtive tear.* He asked Bry what furtive meant. It doesn't matter what furtive means. An Athlone man singing an aria in perfect Italian in 1910, holding his own with Caruso and the like. That's what matters.

There was great confidence in Bry's voice. No arrogance or bullshit. He just knew his stuff and could talk well. The knack that he has for making things seem important, that other people wouldn't think important. It must be something else to be like that in the world.

The coffee and the Count's voice took their chat further home. The Monday nights in Flannery's Bar. The Apparel. The Army Barracks. Watching boats pull into the lock on the Shannon and the gates closing around them. Trying to figure out as boys how the water rose and why it had to rise. Gerald's ma saw *2001: A Space Odyssey* in the old Ritz. 1968. Her father and her grandfather either side of her. The silence in the cinema when the film began. When it ended. On the street outside afterwards. When the deranged monkeys fought in front of the black monolith. Whatever it was, his ma told him fifty years on from the event, it wasn't normal silence.

As the Count sang the last verse, *Si può morir. Si può morir d'amor*, Gerald and Bry went quiet.

The Sanskrit girl kneels down when she hears his name, the blunt taking its toll on her eyes. Bangle sniggers and drops and sits close to the water. Gerald? I was waiting for *Face* or *MadMan* or *Birdhead*. But fucking, *Gerald*!

This accent of the girls is hard to place. The sound of their words is not shaped by anywhere he knows. They pronounce the full of their words. They say them proper.

By the time Bangle passes him the blunt it's been duck-arsed. He pulls some loose burnt bud from the soggy end and snaps a flame at the roach. Once the tip is relit he lungs the smoke long enough to suss it out. The taste and thick texture and body high of an indica. A Kush, perhaps. Although the strong head high says it could be a hybrid. A sativa cross-breed?

Bangle dips her hand into the water. The Sanskrit girl's eyes are closed, her head angled towards the sun. She's a painting. There's no other way to say how perfect she looks. Everything about Bry's illness makes these girls shine like something brand new. The scarring, the medication, the stale bedroom. The gaunt face, and his eyes – when they look back over his shoulder in the bath – blackened from stagnation.

The first boy he kissed was Andy from Brixton. Fabric, London. Double Mitsubishis in the belly and the place full of topless men. Sweat never smelt so good.

Andy tried sucking him off in the jacks but the confinement of the space, the noise, the pills – things like that'd keep a cock down. Especially if the Mitsubishis are speckled. They crushed up another pill on the toilet seat and snorted two lines each. The sting in the nose could never be gotten used to. They washed their hands and faces and walked towards Room One. A volcanic growl rose from beneath the ground. It was like trying to walk across the deck of a boat on choppy seas. The belly turning from the noise. Relax. The floors have built-in bass-bins, Andy shouted back over his shoulder. Tugging him along by the hand towards the noise and heat and sweat.

Andy plugged in the lava lamp in his bedsit when they got back. Threw a bag of skunk and a pipe and a tub of KY on the coffee table and changed into a flowery dressing gown. After they fucked they sat in front of a two-bar gas heater.

Gerald hinted after the last tattoo session in Smithfield – You know, I never stood in that Cobblestone place you were on about. We may mark the occasion so, said Bry.

John Francis Flynn was the first person they saw in there. The Chief, Bry called him. The Chief was playing a tune on two tin whistles strapped together with plumber's tape. A guitar player held his instrument up close to his neck and zoned in on the Chief's hands. He accompanied the tune with interweaving triplets to tie the two whistles together even more. Gerald knew nothing about trad, didn't even know what a triplet was, but he nodded away as Bry whispered into his ear about the workings of the music.

The Chief nodded over at Bry when he finished up the set of reels. The nickname made sense once he put the double-barrel down and stood up to get a pint. The guitar man picked up a fiddle and played his own set of reels. His fiddle sounded drunk. It slowed down and sped up. Short sets of notes would sound good but they'd veer off course before a toe could be tapped, taken off in another direction by something with no proper pulse. Long live Tommie Potts, the Chief said when the set of tunes was over. The elderly man sitting the other side of Gerald raised his glass and brought it to his lips.

John Francis Flynn's new album is on repeat these mornings in the cottage. It's the sort of music that cures things, Bry reckons, or at least makes it easier to get the head around stuff that makes no sense. Bry can get upset eating the breakfast when the Chief sings the Shane MacGowan song. *Oh Kitty, my darling, remember. That the doom will be mine if I stay.* But he perks up afterwards. Looks less loaded.

Where did your friends go? I remember there were more when I spotted yee over the far side. A pair of lookers, them ones, replies Bangle. Which one were ya eyeing? No no, God no. That's not what I meant so it's not. Go on out of that, *Gerald*, there's no denying the two Lisas are a pair of stunners. Why do you think we hang around with them? The Sanskrit girl shakes her head and opens her eyes and throws Bangle a daggery look. Bangle smiles to herself and leans out towards the canal, looking down at her own hand moving back and forth through the water. Two fresh strawberry-sized love-bites on the side of her neck. Without looking up she tells him he'd probably be as old as her father, but she can tell he's not like the other men his age in the town. The older they get, the less they feel they have to hide what they're actually thinking – the dirty fuckers.

Bangle's skin seems something that will never age. Ceramic. A master craftsman made it and set it off with perfectly placed freckles around her nose. She looked so much older from across the canal. It's a girl's face on a woman's body.

Well I didn't mean anything bad when I asked about the other girls. I can guarantee that so I can.

The Sanskrit girl opens her eyes again and studies Gerald. She stands up and takes off her belly top and smells under her arms and throws the top down to Bangle and they both laugh and they've forgotten about the beef they had just seconds ago. She raises her right arm to show the full vertical script running from her oxter to the top of the thick Tommy Hilfiger knicker elastic. *Someone take these dreams away.* That's Ian Curtis, he says. I knew the T-shirt wasn't for show. Yeh? Yeh. Only certain heads actually listen to Joy Division. The rest just buy the T-shirts, like them Ramones ones everyone does be wearing. We're realists so we are, says Bangle. Her eyes in a tight squint. We don't buy into the illusion. You won't find us spending days walking around shopping centres trying on shite clothes and prettying ourselves up. We can talk to the likes of you without being afraid like the two Lisas gone running off home. Well maybe yee should be. What? Afraid? Of you? No no, God no. It's just I used not be afraid neither, that's all. Things can happen so they can. I wouldn't be just trusting people for the sake of it. You're young and all that, I don't know. It just takes time to spot things. It's like the drawing, I suppose, you get more the hang of it as you go along. I like the drawing. The smoke holds things together. Looking after Bry – things'd be tough otherwise.

What's wrong with him? asks the Sanskrit girl. He's going to get better one of the days, says Gerald. Hundred per cent. The surgery and that.

It's just him and Mr Universe back in the cottage at the minute.

What things happen, Gerald? Ah now, he says back. Go on, pushes Bangle. Give us an example of something that could happen, so we'll know exactly what to watch out for.

It's the feeling he gets in the mornings when he wakes up. It starts from the centre of his palms and runs up both arms like a low, pulsing current. Down the chest and into his groin. When he first paid attention to it he had no idea how long it had been there. Could he have been born with such a sensation?

He takes out an indica. A nice body smoke. Because the body remembers everything, Bry reckons. So pay attention to what it's trying to tell you and work with the feelings that arise. But Gerald has no idea how to work with the feelings that arise, so he tokes up when they come. Or the gun comes out and Bry will find somewhere to ink and he'll focus on the pain of the needle.

He passes up to the Sanskrit girl, talking again as the smoke leaves his mouth and nose. Not even remembering what the original question was. I just like art, he says. Anything's a canvas if the art is good. Paper. Concrete. Skin. You've always got skin to work with. Bry specializes in face and neck work.

If you see a decent face in the midlands or up in Dublin, chances are it's one of Bry's.

The Sanskrit girl stands above him. She takes a step closer and he sees the intricate detail in her script. Each word has many colours and there are tiny etchings within the lettering. That is tight work so it is. Bry would love that font – it's like something out of a monk's manuscript. It's only a week old, she says, and moves closer again and kneels down and takes his hand and places the full of his palm on her side between her knicker line and bra. Her skin is new and smooth and plump and her small breasts are goose-pimpled. The lace on her bra is see-through. Her nipples are big, only slightly darker than her skin colour. He jolts and pulls his hand away and looks at the water. Do you mind, Gerald, if I take a closer look at your face?

The child is there, still in her voice. She's no danger. But he can tell himself this till the cows come home and his body will never buy it. The Sanskrit girl runs a thumb down his M.C. Escher. She stretches out his left cheek and the starlings move. It's like they're really flying, she says. Bangle crawls over and stares in close at his face. He doesn't often feel like he's smoked too much, but the heat, the two girls, it's closing in. He goes over the list in his mind. *Cat food for Mr Universe. Bry's medicine. Cat food for Mr Universe. Aloe vera. Epsom salts. Medication. Bry's aloe vera. Cat food, don't forget the fucking cat food again.*

What he likes to do these nights is to rub the aloe vera into Bry's surgery scars. The skin is gotten so tight it looks like it might snap over his shoulder blades in the bath. Sitting behind Bry, he kisses the skin on his back. A decent album playing. Epsom salts, Yankee candles. These recent weeks, since the last operation, he's started to whisper things into Bry. Deep into his back and scars as he applies the gel, deep into his welts. He whispers the way a medicine man might use words to drive something bad from a place.

The Sanskrit girl leans over and kisses Bangle and he watches their mouths and their tongues. The squelchy sounds they make.

The fields lining the canal keep the noise from the town and dual carriageway at bay. A lawnmower is only really noticeable once its engine is cut. He starts telling them about the first night he spent at Bry's place, having to sleep on their sides to fit into the bed. He tells them about Hampstead Heath with Andy. Watching a young man with a golden Wolverhampton Wanderers jersey and a pair of swimming goggles ride a fat old skinhead between two trees. Viva la Wolves, he roared as he came. Small cheers and whistles coming in from different parts of the Heath. We're fucked, Bangle, the Sanskrit girl staring across the water. We are fucked.

Two middle-aged men in black vests walking up the far side of the canal. Their dogs are Rottweilers. A huge semi-circular necklace script on the biggest of the men. Prince, the Sanskrit girl says under her breath. It's Prince. Who's Prince? He's my uncle. He's not your uncle, Katie. He's married to your aunt. That does not make him your uncle. Nor does it give him the right to pull the uncle-talk card, might I add. All he does is work and walk around with that friend of his, what's his face – Greg? Yeh. Silent Greg. All muscles and no mouth. Look at the state of him. Is that bottle tan?

The fuck, Katie?

When he speaks, there's enough depth in his voice to carry it full across the water.

Alright, Prince.

Prince puts his hands behind his head and glances at Gerald. The arms on him look to have served their time on building sites alright. His thick neck.

What are yis talking to that thing for?

He's not a thing, says Bangle. He's a Gerald.

They fall into each other sniggering but it's cut short.

Katie, put your fucking top on. Your mother'll hear about this. And tell Freakshow these two dogs will eat him for breakfast when we get over there.

Relax, Prince. We're just chatting.

Touching up young ones half his age down by the canal. The fuck. What the likes of that'd do to yee if it got half a chance. Look at him with the fucken blue face on him.

Gerald vibrates like he's plugged into something. Running for it would be the option if it weren't for the chong. The heart is telling him to do it anyways. Bry's prescription is in his wallet in the clothes by the water's edge. Bry's prints in his backpack beside Bangle. Medicine, he has to get Bry's medicine.

Prince tells the girls to wait there and starts walking up towards the bridge with the dogs and Silent Greg. Gerald pulls on his top, grabs his stuff. He doesn't look at the girls. He doesn't say goodbye.

II

Some Marks and Spencer workers smoke outside the entrance to the Town Centre, their white shirts and black name tags visible among the shoppers walking through the revolving doors. Another scattering of people sit around the Civic Centre on benches and patches of grass, drinking coffee, chatting in the sun. Not too many, not too bad. The Roma granny around the corner from the post office. One of her regulars hunkered down for the chat, rooting for coins.

There's comfort in the cushion beneath the knees. In the boxes of light that slice in through the glass front of the library. Newspapers, books, photocopies being read. He shuffles back a foot so the John McCormack statue behind him is touching off the soles of his runners, then adjusts the cushion and drags his backpack along. He glances around two or three times – not blocking the way of any pedestrians. No dogs or string vests coming his way.

He displays Bry's prints on the ground around him, props some up against the statue's base. *Original prints by local artist. €5 each.* Directly in front he chalks out a white square on the granite tiles. He lines up his pastels and starts to sketch. His hands still not steady. That script around the man's neck by the canal was probably his name. It looked to have that many letters. He was the sort that might tattoo his own name on his chest.

Gerald doesn't want to look up as someone approaches, but he recognizes the shoes. She stands with her head tilted to one side looking down at the prints.

Hi, Gerald.

Hello, Lizzy.

Are they Bry's?

They are, yeh.

Jesus, you were right, they're incredible. How is he doing?

He's doing fine now, thank you.

I got that aloe vera gel in for you.

Thanks, Lizzy. I'll drop down before I go home.

She buys one of the prints. *Woman in Black Watches Iceberg Calving.* Twenty minutes later he sells another. *Man Rages inside Office Cubicle.* Both 10 x 12s.

His sketch starts off abstract but now two white legs start to dot themselves out. *Beauty Will Save the World* written in blue up the thigh of one. He's never read the Russian writer who said that. It's not his thing. He wants to know nothing more – that one line is enough. He draws the same geometrics on both legs and sells one more print of Bry's within the hour. *The Chief, Smithfield, 2016.*

A young child runs towards him smiling and stops right in front and looks down at the drawing and up at his face and points and says, Smurf!

Smurf! Her mother walks over but doesn't look at Gerald despite the young girl's pointing and smiling. She picks her daughter up and shakes her head and raises her finger and shakes that too. Her lips move like the child is deaf. *No. Danger.* The woman walks towards the library doors and the girl waves back at him over her mother's shoulder.

That library wasn't there when he was growing up. The steps down to the old one by the Shannon was the spot for drinking at the weekend. The night he drank a flagon of cider over there with the two lads from Willow Park. The big one with the mohawk and the good-looking fella with the sallow skin and the undercut. He had always liked the look of them. They had a lot of friends and got mentioned in the Westmeath for scoring goals in the local league. The type of lads that would never usually give him the time of day. But as he was walking by they spoke to him – That a spliff you got on the go there?

They had a couple of smokes. The undercut went up to Val's and came back with three flagons. The mohawk lad pulled out a baggie and they did bumps of coke off Gerald's bank card. The mohawk pulled away after he snorted a large one. Walked over to the railings of the water and grabbed them like he could pull them up out of their foundations. That's the fucking stuff. He had legs that filled and bulged out from his Levi's. Nice the way he wasn't wearing the baggy trousers like everyone else.

More bumps, too close to each other – this was a slow burner, and when it came on, it seemed to hit Gerald harder than the Willow lads. The legs went wonky and he lost track of things for a moment.

When he came back to himself he was sitting down on the wet grass. His flagon spilled beside him. It's grand, they spoke down. We're just able for it. That nosebag's been on the go since Tuesday. It'll wear off in no time.

There was a shine off the two of them when he looked up. The lights from the bridge and street and church all seemed to be pointed in on them like they were on a stage. The mohawk lad had gotten Gerald's weed and was rolling a joint.

They laid out three lines the width of little fingers that ran the length of the bank card. Gerald went first, but the two lads didn't snort theirs. The chat went quiet. That's ketamine, one of them said.

He'd been in K-holes before, and it was decent, but those K-holes had been planned and wanted. He looked up at the two lads as his body started to lie itself down. Two invisible hands mechanically pushing him back. The mohawk carefully sliding the rest of the K back into the baggie. The undercut throwing Gerald's bank card into the water.

The sinking feeling you do be getting as the knowing comes you've done too much and can't go back, just before you go fully under. The two lads, the water, the grass underneath him, the trees swaying, the church steeples above, the street lights. Everything was hostile.

The K had brought great relief in the past. Total detachment from every feeling. It was like being on a weird holiday from himself. But now the sensation was having a straitjacket forced onto the body, onto the mind, the two lads standing over him like crooked prison guards.

Flashes of things woke him briefly, only for him to slip under again straight afterwards.

The feeling of lying in a puddle of water but the strong smell of vomit all around his head.

Being held up against the wall of the library. Pulled over to the railings by the Shannon. If you end up down in Portiuncula, ya bent cunt, you didn't get that off us! Or it'll be the sub-aqua they'll be calling for you next time to rake you out of that water.

He floated above their words, not really understanding anything.

Sirens close then fading away.

The certainty that there was another person, another thing, between him and the two lads. This was the actual one in charge.

The sight but not the sensation of the undercut lad swinging at him and hitting him around the neck or chest. The bigger one dragging him away. Leave him, leave him. There's someone coming.

A late-night cruiser shining its light onshore at him lying on the grass, before speeding off again. No sign of the Willow lads. His body fully paralysed.

When he came to he was standing behind the counter of the video store in St Peter & Paul's Square. The glass from the front window wall was all over the floor. A car swung up around by the church and parked diagonally outside the shop – a D reg Mondeo. The two guards already out and walking towards him. He felt so sober it was like he'd never drank or snorted in his life. On the spot he regretted everything up until that moment in time. But why were the guards walking so casually towards him, swapping torches to try and get both turned on? Why weren't they reacting to him standing behind the cash register of a video shop at 6 a.m. Sunday morning with glass everywhere? It was dark inside the shop. Dark as the K-hole itself.

Keeping the eyes on the guards, he stepped back a few paces to see was there a back way out. His hand found a door handle and he opened it. He slipped in and pulled across the latch. The smell of shite and piss and Domestos. Slow footsteps crunched over broken glass a few metres away. Torch beams sweeping around the edges of the door. Even a heavy breath would give the game away. His eyes as wide as they'd go. The handle was pulled and yanked. The latch held. He left for London a few weeks later.

Bry's uncle is talking to some people outside the post office. He's the type of guard you hear before you see. He'll be over asking questions shortly with that smell of manure off him. The dirt grooved into the slits of his big hands. The crumpled uniform. His hat pitched to one side by a crop of curls.

As he approaches he slides a box of Carrolls from his top pocket and leaves one hanging from the left-hand side of his mouth without lighting it. It bops up and down with his speech.

How's he keeping, Gerald? he says, studying the library windows.

He's good now, improving, thanks, Walter.

Ah I just can't get the head around it meself. A youngish man and hit with such a condition. His mother tells me it's spread to the kidneys. Is there any stopping the fucken thing?

He's going to be fine so he is. We're working on it. The surgery last week removed a big tumour.

I know, I know, but the kidneys, Lord Christ above.

He'll be fine, Walter, so he will, you have to think positive.

Sorry, Gerald. Sorry. I know you're not big on talking straight about these things. Listen, did you get that street licence sorted yet?

It's just with Bry and that, Walter.

Walter takes a step closer and roots out a Clipper from his pocket and lights his Carrolls. He pulls heavy on the cigarette and looks up at the statue of the Count and stays looking at it.

Look, Gerald. Just send in the form is all I'm saying you need do. I'll look after the rest.

I will, Walter, thanks.

That fucking paint is not permanent, is it?

It's just chalk, Walter. The first drop of rain and it'll disappear so it will.

It won't last long so by look of things up there.

Walter looks down to the sketch and angles his head one way then the other.

What is she anyways?

I don't know, Walter.

You're drawing something but you don't know what you're drawing?

I used think you should know what you want to draw before you draw it but not anymore. Works best this way. Bry told me that years back but I only got it recently. I think it has something to do with legs so it has.

Something to do with legs he says. Look, Gerald, just keep your head down and take care of Bry and get that bastard form and we'll get you all set up and legal and you can paint and sell away. The way things is now, you're breaking the law.

I understand, Walter. Thanks.

He starts to give the white thighs the torso of a beetle and a white pin-head and the first drops do start to fall. They line and smudge the drawing, as if looking at it through a rainy windscreen.

III

Close to where he met the Sanskrit girl it stops. He drops his poncho hood and lights another blunt and walks through the post-rain smell. The noise of the canal banks and bushes and trees drinking down the shower. A lot gets missed when the ears are covered with hoods or headphones.

The backpack feels solid, the few bits he had to get pushing in against his back. He taps the side pocket for the box shape of Bry's medicine. A dog barks close by. He looks around and the chest tattoo is the first thing he sees. He was right. *PRINCE.*

Prince and his dog walk towards him like he's not there and he falls back onto his arse. He tries to push himself up but his hands slip on the wet grass. Prince slackens the lead and the Rottweiler is up beside his face. There are dents around the dog's mouth and eyes, like something has taken lumps out of it. The gums heighten with a growl, making its black and yellow teeth even longer. The smell of shite from its breath. Gerald tries to pull back without losing eye contact but there's nowhere to go. He's bolted to the ground. The dog paws at his face.

What would ya have done if I hadn't come along today, ya perv cunt?

Some sharp thing is digging into his spine and he's half winded. Prince yanks the dog's lead and loosens and yanks again. The dog brings lumps of earth with its paws as it's pulled back. Over the dog's head Gerald can see Prince proper for the first time. He raises his arm and points up, a small bit of blood on his fingers from a cut on his nose. Prince slaps away his arm and leans down and looks closer at Gerald and spits.

What did you do to yourself, ya fool?

Gerald reaches and grabs Prince by the shoulders. He takes the back of his head and tries move it towards his. Prince leans back to balance himself, holding the dog. Gerald snatches at the lead hand and pulls it in and sucks on Prince's thumb. He doesn't have it in his mouth for long, but long enough to suck the length of it and move his tongue around it, and there's a taste of dog and construction and hand cream and he gives it a small bite before Prince hits him with his other hand and Gerald lets go. Prince staggers back, falls on his arse. His face scrunches up looking at his own thumb. Ya sick fuck ya.

Gerald moves his head down to the left to let the blood flow away from his eye. The Rottweiler walks towards the water, dragging his lead behind him. He enters the canal up to the neck, goes perfectly still. The three of them panting.

Gerald rolls over onto his side and sits up. He roots out another pre-rolled. A white widow. Cagily, he lights it up, offers it over to Prince, holding his own right hand steady with his left to control the shake. Prince doesn't look at him but Gerald leaves it down on the grass, the smoke rising up between the two of them.

The dog stares up at Prince, waiting to see what he'll do. Gerald checks for the boxes from the chemist as Prince picks up the smoke. He puffs and coughs, looking out at the dog in the water. He smokes a bit more once the coughing stops. He doesn't look over at Gerald. He doesn't pass it back.

HONEY BROWN

You've got ninety-two on the clock today, Honey Brown. You've got macular degeneration. A 1960s ferry from Rosslare to Fishguard saw you put five decades in over the water before coming home. Hybridity in your accent. Black glasses covering your white-filmed eyes.

You have a suite on the top floor of the Windview Private Nursing Home, on the fringes of your birthplace – Elphin, County Roscommon, Percy French country. Beside the bed is a good-sized workbench for the Singer and plenty of space for Oyster to sleep. It was worth it to pay extra for the room with the best view of the windmill. Shapes and colours could still be made out when you arrived.

The endless run of deep green behind the windmill's sails. And on certain days, it could multiply. More windmills would rise out of the ground, either side of the original. Turning back into your room to try shake off the feeling, the one that made you clench your teeth and curl down your toes, the new windmills would appear on the wall over your bed. But they were much smaller up there. Oyster would need a rub to calm him down.

You pull on your Gobi cashmere tights this morning, a subtle 92 on each instep. Your carer insisted on being your eyes yesterday while you embroidered the numerals. She patched up your punctured hands afterwards and said the work came out perfect, even though your fingertips told you one of the 9s looked more like a 7. To go with the tights, the white woollen maxi and the Lilysilk blouse. You want to look your best. Not so much for the birthday party, but for the noon appointment with Doctor Ann over the MRI results. You know many in this home who don't even remember the MRI that confirmed their darkest fears. That left them in a void in a room on their own.

At breakfast over your toast and juice and Complan, you tell Dorothy Reagan the feel of the loose pleated skin draping from your neck reminds you of the scarlet satin curtains from your first flat on the Essex Road, not far from Highbury and Islington on the Victoria Line, even closer again to Angel on the Northern Line. You rented that flat off the Jamaican lady who sold slimming tablets to Esther. Esther was there on the back of her ballet scholarship to the Royal Academy of Dance. She was the reason you moved to London. Not that it hadn't always been the vision, but Esther was the fuel. She was the confidence.

I saw Esther smoke at eleven, Dot. Eleven. She was rebel from day one. I met her in Claremorris at a *feis* in 1957. She took gold in three categories. I heard my mother tell her mother that that girl was a born dancer. I heard Esther's mother tell my mother that it was the ballet Esther really wanted. Esther nodded at me when this was said and took a drag of her mother's Woodbine without anyone noticing. I don't know how she held in the cough. I nodded back. Esther and myself and our mothers became *feis* friends. It was the Fleadh Cheoil in Boyle in 1966 where she told me about her scholarship to the Royal Academy. I told her about my boutique dream.

I was a checkout woman, Honey, my whole life. Kelly's shop. Kelly's supermarket. Kelly's Londis. Same till all the way along.

You were happy, Dot?

Knowing my place was enough.

Did you never want to travel?

I never had the feet for travelling.

I always loved being at home too, wherever that was. Would you believe my flat on the Essex Road was close to the Arsenal Football Club?

If you say it, Honey, I'm believing it.

Saturday afternoons. Sketching out designs or taking in a skirt, with red and white flowing by my window, that's what I really enjoyed. And when Esther and the girls went out, I stayed in. I just adored Saturday nights at home, even when I was young. People tell me I kept it clean all my life, that's why I've reached such a great age, but I never took to that description of myself. Clean. The opposite of clean is dirty and Esther was anything but dirty. She was home. She was a born dancer.

I was a bingo person, Honey. Fridays and Saturdays. Second row with Janice Cox. Elphin Community Centre. Into the big smoke then, Roscommon Town, first Friday of the month for the Snowball. Did you know Janice, Honey?

She was a dancer, Dot?

All the Coxs could dance. Janice'd be no different.

Did you like a dance, Dot?

I was never allowed a dance and it never bothered me only it did my feet no good.

You only went to the Northern Soul dance halls once. It was that same summer you lost Esther to her Mancunian boyfriend and to the amphetamine pills he used to duct-tape behind the side panel of his Vespa. It's as if a force is drawing your skin and stomach inwards each time you picture Esther's stick-thin figure disappearing around the corner on the back of the Vespa, leaving you alone outside Mike Gold's dance hall on Dean Street. She was going nowhere with that boyfriend, but not wanting to upset the apple cart, nothing was said. You even helped her find her slimming tablets when she lost them. But turning a blind eye to the Benzedrine she kept stashed beneath a floorboard in the bathroom, that's a hard one to forgive. Dorothy Reagan says she's always wanted a spin on a Vespa. You say you were more of a Lambretta woman yourself.

The carers come in and Dorothy tells you they're hanging the birthday bunting. There's rumours of a big cake, and a gramophone and some 78s have been borrowed from the antiques woman in Boyle town. All the fuss tenses you up. You rub your neck again, massaging skin and muscle. You suggest to Dorothy to move next door to the day room. Dorothy Reagan gently, so as not to startle you like some of the carers often do, reaches over and takes your arm and puts Oyster's harness in your hand.

Your day-room armchairs are in the farthest corner from the television, beside the big bay window, looking out on the garden and the vegetable patch. The gardener clipping the hedge by the main road, her un-oiled wheelbarrow bringing the cuttings to the compost pile once the first pats of rain hit the window. The smell of her Silk Cut Purple when she takes a break. Dorothy Reagan touches your arm again – Glasses, please, Honey, small smudge on left lens. She places the glasses back in your hand when she's finished.

Thanks, Dot. You're very good to me.

Keeps me sharp, Honey Brown. Watching out for the little things. Last thing I want is to end up like you-know-who over there.

Sharp is a good plan, Dot. Actually, have I mentioned I've an appointment today with Doctor Ann?

Rather you than me. I haven't seen her ladyship in six months, and long may it last.

Well it's about my – you know, Dot, the little things I do be seeing.

Say no more, Honey.

It's just that, funnily enough, they started five years ago to the day, on my eighty-seventh.

Remember I arrived here that year and I could still make out shapes? What I could see, mixed with the sounds I could hear, it let me build a good enough picture of what was happening. But sitting before the cake that day, everything vanished. I saw a lake spreading out in all directions, lovely sky-blue water, and I felt as if I were floating over it in my armchair in pure silence. I was gone before *for she's a jolly good fellow*. I was back before the last *hip hip hooray*. Yet everything was much darker, and within the week, my sight was gone.

Verrucas. That's the cross I've been carrying since I was a young woman. You'll never see Dot Reagan in a set of sandals. That's what happens when you don't dance, you know. Verrucas. The checkout suited me that way.

Well I think you could still make a great dancer, Dot. There's a lovely sound to your gait.

Them two feet could shut down dance halls, believe you me.

Parts of us just close down as we move on, Dot, isn't it? Your feet. My eyes – they couldn't find a diagnosis for the longest of times you know. Not for the hallucination part anyways. But then Doctor Ann, she arranged for that eye specialist to come and visit. Do you remember that chap, Dot?

The lad with the mouth?

Oh and we shouldn't be laughing. Just he had that bit of a lisp and every second word out of his mouth started with an S. It was almost like he thought that if he tried enough of them his luck would change.

A Belmullet man, was he not, Honey? North Mayo? Not that I've ever been but I've heard they're all the same up that direction. Something to do with the moving statues. Or was that in Tipperary?

It's perfectly acceptable, Ms Brown, he said to me, for the visually impaired to experience intense visions as their eye mechanism fails. It's not something to be ashamed of.

That's Belmullet alright.

I'm not ashamed, Doctor, I said back to him.

Dead right, Honey. Tell them nothing.

When Dorothy shuffles across the day-room floor to go the toilet, you sit in her seat a moment. The rain pat pats the window, the wind sweeps and scrapes the leaves along the path. A section of the upholstery feels flimsy beneath your hands and you tell the staff that this arm is close to a tear.

It might be worth uncovering the Singer at some stage today for a dust and oil. The rhythm of the presser foot off the needle plate is calming. Your right thumb is nearly always thimbled. There's something about sitting in your room with garments in hand and imagining the raw materials that went into making them. Things that don't naturally arrive that way on this earth but are shaped beautiful through craft.

But alone too long in this day room, the smell takes your attention. As nice as the cleaners and the carers are, they can never quite get rid of it. There's solace in that you yourself nearly always make it to a bathroom on time. Any accidents are hidden and cleaned before anyone has a chance to notice. A lot of the work now is about them never getting a nappy on you. Good news at Doctor Ann's today, that would be a blessing, because amongst the day-room smells are the day-room murmurings. The Beirne man asking what time dinner is at, even though he's had it the same time every day since you arrived. Mrs Cregg in the corner opposite complaining about the child that never visits and the same woman never even had a child. That Lavin man asking one of the cleaners who that woman is sitting beside him. That's your sister, Frank, she tells him, as she always does. Oyster gets to his feet and reverses into your knees, standing guard.

A tap on your left hand and you take a breath like you've emerged from water. Your body soon relaxes again listening to Dorothy's strong, sharp voice. She helps you move into your own seat and

Oyster settles down and sits by your feet. Dorothy asks one of the carers would there be any chance of some Percy before dinner. You and Dorothy would have grown up with Percy French in your houses. Your grandmother hummed his tunes to you as a child. There's quietness when the nurse puts the song through the day-room Tannoy, but the chorus you both sing aloud.

> *With a toot on the flute*
> *And a twiddle on the fiddle-oh*
> *Hopping in the middle*
> *Like a herrin' on the griddle-oh*
> *Up, down, hands around*
> *And crossing to the wall*
> *Sure hadn't we the gaiety*
> *At Phil the Fluter's ball*

Could we have made it as opera singers?

We still might.

You've never told Dorothy Reagan about finding Esther in the bath early that Sunday morning in 1968 – not about her sunken eyes or her vivid descriptions of the things only she could see in the bathroom. And not a single word has been uttered about what caused her psychosis – the black bombers, the purple hearts, the PCP, the slimming tablets. That would be a betrayal. Esther swore to you that morning she had gotten the lead in *Swan Lake* and you just couldn't bear to remind her that she'd lost her scholarship the month previous. By the lightness of her body as you helped her out of the water, it was clear before any of the doctors or police intervened that that wasn't the real Esther. The real Esther was the weight missing.

The best thing to do was to avoid music for months after she was committed. Gloria Jones's 'Tainted Love' was the song that was blaring from the wireless when you found her in the bath and you never wanted to hear it again. The following month you took another temping job on the Clerkenwell Road and lasted six months before you went towards what was yours since you were a child and old enough to fabricate dreams. The boutique in Soho. You went in an unpaid trainee. A tea maker. A runner. A window dresser. A sales assistant. The place was yours within the decade. You renamed it Threads of Esther.

Doctor Ann's office always smells of freshly watered plants. Jasmine. Rich Italian coffee. You don't know how she does it, but apart from the chapel, it's the only room that doesn't smell like a nursing home. You shake as she goes through your file, the sharp sound of the pages turning feels like cuts to your mind.

Your MRI results are back, Honey. You have nothing to worry about. I've highlighted the important parts in case you want someone to read them to you.

Thank you, Doctor Ann.

And I've been speaking to my colleagues in psychiatry. The last day you seemed a little concerned that maybe there was some psychosis connected with this?

Well, I wouldn't be saying that out loud to too many people now Doctor, but yes, the hallucinations can be a little scary to be honest, and I don't hear of anyone else having them.

Can I ask you some questions about them, Honey?

You can.

Do you interact with them – the hallucinations? Do the people in them notice you are there watching them?

They don't, no. There wouldn't be any interaction.

They are more like movies than presences, isn't that what you said before?

It's like I'm watching something as opposed to taking part in it, yes.

And how were they before your sight fully went?

Well, I saw flowers grow from the chaplain's head one day in the breakfast room. Orchids and wood lilies. When I looked away and out the window, I could see the same flowers growing from a cloud in the sky, but they were much bigger up there.

This is normal, Honey. This is classic Charles Bonnet syndrome. You are definitely not going mad. It's just your brain telling you what to see instead of your eyes.

As in, Doctor?

As in once your eyes stop picking up what's there, your brain starts to compensate for the lack of input.

Would I be improvising?

We could say that, yes.

But I suppose there is a feeling that, well it sounds silly to say. Especially as I don't have the belief the others do.

Go on, Honey. I'm listening.

It's just that I sometimes think my blindness is me getting what I deserve. And the visions that come, although some are very beautiful and they allow me to briefly see, they can also be quite severe. Like I am being punished for things I did or didn't do.

Eyesight deterioration is extremely common for your age group, and you're also one of the oldest residents here. The fact you don't suffer from any other serious illnesses is a testament to the life you've lived. You don't get punished for living a good life like that, Honey.

The chapel is a place you'd rarely visit while you still had sight, but you go there daily now – for the quiet, not the belief. And in between services and confessions, funeral masses and choir rehearsals, eyes closed, in dark glasses, sometimes tailored white blouses, sometimes lime-green pleated ankle-length skirts, Oyster at your side, you sit alone in the front pew and what you see is nothing like you ever saw when you had sight. Close-ups of extinct exotic animals that the BBC would kill for. Boats made of light floating across seas of wool. A lone cashmere goat strolling across the Gobi Desert – wool intact. A single file of people ascending a blue velvet escalator with no banisters. They wear Mongolian yak wool robes. Red saris. Mohair suits.

And these hallucinations come and go every day, often in the early afternoon or at night before sleep. They come mostly good, but you know if it's a bad one you are about to see and you've had that feeling all morning. It petrifies you when you see her. The young woman sitting on the floor in the corner of a dimly lit room. You open your eyes but she is still there, crouched where the altar would be in the chapel, holding her knees up to her chest. Her mouth is sewn shut and she starts to claw at the thick stitches that bind one lip to the other. Her eyes are making the actions of screaming but no sound comes. She desperately wants to say something and you want to help her but this is a movie. This is Charles Bonnet syndrome. This is not real. She can't see you so she can't exist. You close your eyes and look to where the ceiling of the chapel was and up where you remember the stone angels to be. She's hovering up there, looking down at you.

Oyster reverses into your legs and growls. This too will pass, you say out loud, as Doctor Ann had said to say when things got very difficult. This too will pass, but it doesn't. You grab Oyster's harness and tap your foot and let your body move back and forth to the rhythm. You sing so lightly and slowly it comes out a whispered lullaby:

Are ye right there, Michael? Are ye right?
Do ye think that you can get the fire to light?
Oh, an hour you'll require
For the turf it might be drier

And it might now, Michael
So it might.

Eyes open. Waiting. Nothing comes. Eyes closed. Open again. Same. Some faint sparks on the periphery of your vision – for once you're glad it's only darkness you see. You settle Oyster down with a strong rub of his neck. The door creaks open behind you and your whole body begins to tremble again until you hear her voice and feel her gentle touch on your shoulder.

They've rang the dinner bell, Honey. That new man from Creeve is eyeing up our seats. I'm thinking we should make our way down.

After a lunch of mashed potato and vegetable purée and overdone cod, with Dorothy slipping her portion onto your plate thinking you won't notice, there's the same feeling you had before you went to the chapel. The sick stomach. The sensation something awful might happen. You hope you don't have another episode, overexcitement can bring them on, so you try to take your mind off all the birthday commotion. But you feel the girl with the stitched lips is still close by. Sitting beside you, she could be. Because they can call them complex hallucinations and stick a fancy French name on them, but you're not daft. You reach out and find Dorothy's hand and squeeze her fingers and she squeezes back and tells you not to worry. No one's looking at you. They're all fixated on the dog and the bunting. She explains the staff are now dimming the lights. You prepare yourself as best you can. The skin beneath your neck is good to hold onto. Long slow breaths. It's difficult not to grind your teeth.

The ninety-two candles appear as a faint radiance emerging from black-hole dark, but you smell the burning wax. The heat rises and warms your face. You smell the melting fudge they used to ice the words *Happy Birthday Honey Brown*. You sense the smiles from the staff and carers and other residents, even the ones who don't know where they are in the world anymore, but they still recognize a birthday cake when they see it. You wonder where all the lost memories go when they go.

You said last week to Doctor Ann that we should sit more and listen to each other. You'll always feel both sides of the water within you, moving you. Sitting around with friends and carers, the texture of Esther's voice is there, somewhere in the chorus of *and so say all of us*. Deep breath. Blow. The heat is still there. Blow again. You make your wishes. Protection for the girl in the chapel. Protection for yourself from the girl. The hope is you'll never see her again. Dorothy's strong breath pushes the smell of burning candles back in your direction. I'm just getting the last few stragglers, Honey, she says.

You smile and nod and say thank you, thank you. Someone says, We love you Honey Brown, and you squeeze your eyes closed. The slicing of the cake makes you wince, the steel of the knife scraping the glass tray like a nail on a window. The sharp scrape of ceramic on ceramic as the plates get served. You reach out for the harness and tap your toe to the Percy French 78 somebody has put on the gramophone. You hope no one gives Oyster any of the cake.

PATTERNS

Martin fed on books about nature and lost tribes. His picture book about the Emberá was an early favourite. Their jagua face tattoos. Boys and girls his own age inked from the lips down to the chin. Little beard men, he would say, and when I sat beside him to take a peek, the sound of his breath and his clumsy turning of the page was all I heard. So still he was, sometimes. Like he'd left his small body to go live in this other world.

Martin was glued to my father at the time, us all living together on the Sligo coast in the house we'd eventually inherit. Dad always spoke to Martin as if he were a grown-up, even when he was just a toddler, and Martin spoke back just the same.

Robbing his expressions and throwing them out to anyone within earshot.

They chatted about the designs in my father's old buildings. It always brought him great peace, especially after he retired. He could mesmerize Martin with stories from the bigger projects, and Martin would close his eyes and imagine the symmetry and the geometry. The brutalists and the minimalists.

After one of their library visits, Martin landed back with *Patterns of the Amazon*. He spent weeks running his fingers over each page. Tracing carefully the tattooed designs that lined the faces and bodies of the people who stared out hard at him from the page. When he came to the section on the Shipibo, he began tracking out lines on my face and down my neck and across my chest and arms. Pointing back and forth between my blank skin and that of a Shipibo elder.

Same. Tom same, book same. His voice high pitched, but with a timbre already closer to my father's than my own. I nodded back to him.

Yes, son, same. We're all the same. But he became more insistent and used both hands, one on the book to trace a design on the elder's face, lines that looked like a plan for a geometric maze. His other he used to trace an exact copy onto my face.

Tom same, he said, woman same.

Martin never lost interest in the weekly book hunts. It gave my father great go, even after he started to fail. Libraries and bookshops and markets. Simon Community shops and St Vincent de Pauls. When Dad's energy levels were good, the two of them could be on the early train to Dublin by the time myself and Kate were up. And it didn't matter if they disappeared the odd weekday. We've homeschooled Martin since Senior Infants. He doesn't know how to sit down, we were told at the first parent–teacher meeting. He rarely looks at the other kids, but when he does, he won't stop staring at them. We keep finding him in the toilet looking at himself in the mirror and touching his face.

Once Dad became too ill to leave the house, Martin insisted on taking more time off from his lessons to be with him. He would spend the day reading out loud on the bed, and if my father couldn't take it, Martin would lie beside him and flick through pages of one of their photo books. I came across him marking out lines on my father's face early one Friday morning. A very light white crayon. Martin had started at the tip of my father's nose and drawn fractal shapes out until the whole face was covered. When it was finished, it looked like a close-up of a snowflake. By the Monday Dad was gone.

A week later Martin was still upstairs beside the empty bed. Kate begged him time and time again to come down, but he insisted he had to stay around in case Grandad hadn't gone anywhere yet.

You're too young to be thinking like that, Martin. Come down.

I'm in double figures now, Kate – no more messing about.

I listened outside the door to him talking away in there. It was like he was trying to resurrect my father through the use of his old sayings. There's no straight lines in nature. A good design is like a frozen tune. Be careful how you shape a building because it'll end up shaping you.

He came down the stairs on the Wednesday and sat between us. He picked up one of his new books and started to read.

Martin was rocking himself from side to side on our bed a few days after Dad's first anniversary, simultaneously reading *Habits of Asturian Wildlife* and *Walking with Bears*. Kate was checking us in for our 6.30 a.m. Aer Lingus flight from Dublin to Oviedo. Through the bedroom window I saw her trying to get Martin to swap one of his books for *Diary of a Wimpy Kid*. Martin looked at her like she had lost her mind. I was fuming. I said nothing. I had snacks and microphones to organize. I settled on olives and cheddar cheese for supper and decided the paired Audio Technica condensers were the way to go. The ATs are compact, sturdy, good in the field. I had planned to travel alone. Time to think. Less time to argue. More time to focus on the work, but it was Martin who changed my mind.

What's this big job I'm hearing about, Tom? he said from the door of my garden studio, shortly after I'd told Kate of my plans. His voice was now lower. It still lacked real bottom end but the mids and highs were there. They could have been cut straight from a childhood recording of his grandfather, especially when he used one of Dad's sayings like this.

It's a documentary on Spain's wild bears, Martin. A what-if kind of thing. What would happen if they were ever to come back? I've gotten the foley gig for it so I'm flying out for a week to grab some field recordings in the area and meet with the producers and talk about the sound design.

They've gone nowhere, them bears, he said to me, they've just gotten clever. Give me a minute.

He slapped his passport onto my workbench when he came back and Kate walked in behind him and smiled. Martin kept it serious as usual but looked me right in the eye, which he rarely does.

You'll be needing backup on this one, Tom, and I want none of this lone-wolf talk. Now, first things first, what are we thinking weapon wise – condensers? Dynamics? Or will we chance the large clip-ons? We can knock the fuckers out with a couple of tranks and then pin mics onto them before they come to.

Martin, language!

I'm going alone, Martin. You'll stay here with your mother.

I'm a field soldier, Tom. Kate, will you talk sense into this husband of yours?

When he spoke like this my skin often reacted as if it were the sound waves from my father's words hitting it and not my son's. It was like having the two of them there together again. He'd always be able to get around me if he went on speaking like that.

Bedtime, Martin. It's midnight and you're twelve.

Boys of my age are already considered men in some tribes, Kate.

Kate managed to hold a straight face long enough for him to fall into her. He was getting sleepy, already starting to make the *tick* sound with his tongue. I stood out into the garden and held up his passport. Kate turned around as she got to the back door with him and I waved it about. She led him inside.

Walking the trail back to our cottage from the nearest village, our second night in Asturias, Martin stopped midway through a field. Listened. Ran off into the waist-high grass and knelt down out of sight.

They're singing to us to, Tom. Kate. Listen. They're serenading us so they are.

Who's singing to us, Martin?

Those crickets and that rufous nightingale up at the top of that dragon tree.

I'd call it chirping myself, Martin, I said to him. But I suppose it's their little way of singing.

There's only one way to sing, Tom, and those lads are at it. All you have to do is slow down those chirping sounds inside your head and you'll hear it. And for someone of your sound-engineering talents, this shouldn't be rocket science.

OK, son, we'll take your word for it.

Don't 'OK son' me. My name is Martin James and I'd never lie to you two people – but those crickets and that fucken bird are singing to us.

Martin, language. Please!

Sorry, Kate. But that's all they do. Singing is the only thing that gets that bird out of the nest in the morning. I've read all about him. And it's the thing that keeps them crickets up all night. Why can't you hear it too?

I doubled back after midnight. I placed two mini-tripods in the patch of grass where Martin had stopped and I mounted the mics and positioned them in an XY set-up to capture the full spatial expanse. I set the recorder to take audio at 96kHz. High input gain. I socked both mics with windshields and cabled them to the recorder with the luminescent XLRs and previewed the signal on my Sennheisers. I wasn't sure if the crickets had clocked off for the night, as all was clear and quiet, but I tweaked the input level down a notch in case strong winds picked up, and hit record. I repositioned the mics once more so that one was closer to the dragon tree and then just lay down in the field. Once I stopped making sounds, the crickets started. I heard noises that could pass as sucking sounds, slow, far-off referee whistles, very light and soothing alarm clocks, but I heard no discernible song. The bird weighed in and out with time and all went quiet again. I lay and listened to the light breeze and distant sea.

When I woke it wasn't far off dawn, and by the time I packed up and made it back to the cottage, Martin was up and waiting.

What kind of an hour would you classify this as, Tom?

It's an hour that you should still be sleeping, Martin.

I do me best thinking in the small hours, Tom, but I'd appreciate if we kept that between ourselves.

It'll go no further, Martin, said Kate, as she walked out of the bedroom behind us. Now, what'll we get up to today?

We'll do the exact same thing as yesterday, Kate.

A double day it is so, Martin.

If yee don't mind.

We don't mind, love.

Kate, that's slack so it is – the name's Martin.

Understood, Martin.

Same food?

And same spot on the beach, same walk home.

It's fierce important, he said, and then went quiet in himself. The left eye began to go and his mouth ticked. He sometimes joked he was imitating a little animal he'd seen on a BBC documentary. One that would find its way out of trouble using sonar. We left him at it a minute to see would it settle, but his eyelids started to wingbeat and his head rose, like he was being charmed. He started to drool.

Tell us more, Martin, Kate said as she knelt down in front of him. Explain to us what's fierce important.

Kate had a way to refocus him on the thing that set him off so he could put the brakes on. On the good days he could still himself in an instant. I took a deep breath and put my arms back down by my sides. I hadn't realized I'd been standing there like a zombie, as if my outstretched arms could have fixed him without touching him. We don't panic or go too close to him anymore when he's in full flow. Seeing him being sedated like an animal once by paramedics, that changed our tune on how we react to him.

He moved over to the rear window of the cottage and pointed up towards the mountains. Imagine, he told us, there's a man leaping around alone up there. Total random moves. Dressed in rags. Hopping from side to side like he's trying to shake off a swarm of invisible bees. What do we have here?

We have a complete lunatic on our hands, Martin.

OK, Tom. But now imagine beside that man a woman. And another man. A whole go of people dressed in the same rags and moving the same moves in perfect time with each other. What do we have now?

The beach was full of sunbathers. No wind, low tide. I'd been there the evening we arrived to capture quiet samples for the opening scene of the documentary. It was calm and peaceful then. But daytime meant lifeguards humming around in their electric buggies. Kids shouting at their kites to take flight. Reggaeton and dancehall basslines booming out from the ice-cream hut on the sand's edge, and the *pit* and *pat* of wooden-racket tennis was a constant. Our spot from the previous day was taken but we stood close by and waited for a young couple to leave. Martin approached them and started chatting like they were friends, something he inherited from his grandfather. I'd find it difficult to pull such a stunt. Have yee got names, yee have? he said.

Martin's lower lip pushes out when he's starting to get excited or inquisitive. That can lead to the fast blinking, maybe the drooling. I saw the man smirk at his girlfriend and Kate grabbed my hand and pulled me towards her. I'd gone in over the checkout at a lad in Lidl a few weeks back. Martin had challenged him on the price of spuds and said they were cheaper during the famine and then his right eye started to twitch and he ticked and as we were trying to settle him down, the checkout lad starting giving his colleagues the eye to look over at Martin.

You can't do that, Tom, Kate said to me outside in the car park as we were loading the messages into the boot. Imagine you had connected?

What am I meant to do? Stand by and let them all laugh at him?

Actually, you're dead right, Tom, she said in her voice that she used to get her best points across. Beat them all into a pulp with your big manly hands and head off to jail and let them take Martin off us. That's definitely the best plan. Good man.

I returned a squeeze to her hand on the beach and let her know I was with her. We'd do things her way. Martin looked at the young man and asked him had he a name or not. Stuart was his name. And María Jose was his girlfriend. The young woman smiled at Martin and glanced away to the sea. Martin kept looking at her and when she looked back her smile became forced and nervous. Martin stared at her bikini-topped chest, at her flattened bronze belly. The ticks started. Then his eyes. I spotted a large lady on a deckchair off to one side, letting on she was taking a selfie. I could see she had Martin in focus on her screen. The girl leaned forward and hugged herself into a nauseous shape. The young man's smirks were gone and the girl tugged his togs to go. Martin leaned over to one side and his head tilted back beyond his neck like he had a bad creak. His stomach sucked inwards, all his ribs visible. When he started to drool we walked over and crouched beside him. The couple got to their feet and the boyfriend hurried their things together. In fairness to the lad, he turned and apologized as they left.

We got Martin speaking and calmed his body and baby-wiped the drool from his chin and chest. I spotted the phone rise once more over the deckchair beside us – That fucking thing is going into the water if you try it again. We're not running a circus here.

She didn't look around at me but upped and left. A pair of lifeguards came by.

We can help?

No, thank you, everything is fine.

But the *chico*. You need doctor?

The *chico* is the fucken soundest, thanks.

They sauntered away and left us be. I got Martin to lie back and gaze up at the clouds. Kate fussed over paper cups and plates. Orange juice and Spanish tortilla with spinach as we had had the day before at the same time. But she was on edge. I gave her a nudging look.

What was happening with that girl, Martin?

I'm supposing a woman of your intuition noticed something about her too, Kate.

I didn't notice anything about her, Martin.

OK. Well, it doesn't matter now.

It matters, Martin. What did you see when you looked at that girl? Why did you both start to seem sick?

It was just her belly. It was a big mess. Like all the colours were mixed up and the patterns were melting.

I made time to work each night between midnight and 2 or 3 a.m. Martin and Kate safe in bed and with everything that quiet, I'd shake off what I could of the day and try and find some flow. The documentary was in more or less its final edit stage. Visually it was humming, subtle effects had been applied, mastered with a slick sheen over everything. Tasty transition work. But seeing as there was such a heavy dependency on CGI, all sounds were to be added in post. I had built up a decent foley catalogue from the beach samples in the evenings. I'd made field recordings before I left Strandhill. The rest I could record and compose on the spot.

The opening scene showed a wild female bear making her way up from the Cantabrian sea, towards the viewer, as if she'd just landed onshore for the first time. The bear walked in silence until every pixel on my plasma monitor was darkened by her outline. I hit the space bar and freeze-framed the image. Ran my fingers down along the screen, down over her short rounded ears and the dish-shaped profile between the eyes and the end of her nose. I tried to hear the sounds that I needed to bring this creature fully to life and, as CGI as it was, the bear held a stare of true wildness. Can a machine be wild? There's one for Martin to ponder when he's older. Or maybe in the morning over his Coco Pops.

We need to talk but I don't want you to get angry, OK?

We were eating a late dinner in the cottage, a couple of days after the beach incident, and by the time I heard her say *OK* like that, I was flaming.

The doctor.

Don't.

He's one of the best in the business.

Exactly, the business.

The trial he told us about before. It's worth a try, she said.

Even if we wanted to, Kate, the price of that stuff – what are they calling it?

Exanorm, I think.

Exanorm? Good fuck. They could do with some subtlety in the marketing department.

Kate reached over and touched my knuckles. They were whitened from the squeeze I had on the fork. I put it down and looked over at Martin's dinosaur flip-flops.

Maybe I got the name arseways, Tom. Does it really matter? Loads of kids have to take medicine. That's just a fact. It's not that big of a deal if Martin is one of them.

Loads of *sick* kids take medicine, Kate. Martin is not sick.

People laugh at him. They take photos and stare at him.

Let them stare.

This medicine, Tom. Look. Jesus, I don't know.

She looked around to see was he about before she spoke again. Her voice a lot lower.

The only thing I'm certain of is that I am not comfortable. I don't want Martin to be seeing these things anymore. And these people stare at him like he's a freak. It's just that simple for me. Jesus, if you think about it. It's just not right, those things.

Patterns. It's OK to say what they are, Kate. Try it. *Patterns*. Go on, after me now – *Our son sees patterns on people.*

I handed her a tissue and walked over to the window and looked up at the red sky over the mountains.

It'll just help him, Tom. It won't change his personality. And the doctor says he'll take Martin on free of charge as part of the trial. What have we got to lose?

I wanted to say OK, let's do it, just to make her feel better, but the words wouldn't come. I hunkered down and started to line up all our shoes by the door.

We can't guinea-pig him out, Kate. That's what this is. Some doctor with notions who probably wants to write a paper about weird kids and a new drug. That's the only reason he's offered it for free. Fuck him and fuck his medicine. I'll go and live in a cave with Martin if I have to.

And I'll stand at the door of that fucking cave, Tom, but Martin will still be seeing the same things he sees everywhere else. Can you handle a lifetime of that? Have you never wondered what he sees when he looks at us?

Behind us Martin stood in the hallway. Sick down his front and holding his pants with both hands from behind. We said nothing. In the bathroom we stripped and showered him down. I crouched and held him in my arms while Kate ran a bubble bath.

Kate, Tom, he said while looking between the two of us at a point on the wall. Sorry for the mess.

It's been a while since I left a load like that in the underpants. I've a bit too much mileage on the clock now for that sort of carry-on.

You're twelve, Martin.

I'd be considered a man in some cultures, would you believe, Kate.

You've mentioned that alright.

Did you hear us arguing, Martin. Is that what set you off?

I heard nothing, Tom. I had the ears plugged with the 25 dB filters and I was reading my book. But I saw the argument.

How did you see the argument, Martin, if you were reading your book in bed?

Well, I saw the air get crooked around my head. And when I looked at the door, the hallway was funny looking. Like it had got too small to walk through.

We filled in some hot water and let out some of the cold. I added more bubble bath and Kate shampooed his hair and scrubbed under his arms. Neither of us had a response for him. We mightn't be able to understand everything he says but we understand how to mind him. All we want to do is mind him. The bathroom filled with steam so we opened the window and turned off the tap. When we stopped, we all three just sat and listened to the sounds of nature coming in from the outside. The light breeze. The sea. The distant sounds of crickets a few fields over.

For the bear's footstep foley, I used field recordings of my own steps from the beach back home in Strandhill. The Sligo sand is a lot wetter and denser than the Spanish stuff and the acoustics came out much sharper and deeper and the raw material needed less processing. I copied in my lefts and rights and synched them to the bears. Pitched them down by 25 per cent and started to get a nice deep *thud*. I ran them through a heavy kick-drum compressor, boosted the lows around 110 Hz and added a gated reverb with a medium release envelope so that each step's echo was felt and heard for miles around this imaginary landscape.

As the machine-bear slouched towards the screen, I listened to the monstrous footsteps and started to plan the sounds for the roar and the breath. But gazing into those wild digital eyes, I was taken over by fear and had to turn it off.

Kate and myself sat and watched in darkness. Both wearing cans to not wake Martin. The files from my SD card loaded into the wave editor and filled the middle of the screen from left to right. The falls and troughs and flatlines as the audio etched its way into life, and when it had loaded up, we listened back. The rustling of my hands repositioning the mics. The noise of my body lying down in the long grass. The crickets beginning to *cricket*. The bird joining in. My mouth beginning to snore and the very calming sounds of the Cantabrian sea at night. I routed the pitch of the audio to the midi jog-wheel on my workbench. I lifted one side of the headphones away from Kate's ear and pointed to the device.

If you turn that wheel to the left, Kate, it'll pitch the file down.

As in?

It'll do what Martin says we need to do to hear if these lads can sing or not.

Bit by bit the crickets got deeper and slower but all it sounded like was deep and slow crickets. I nodded for her to turn it more. A hundred times slower than normal and still no singing. We both moved closer to the screen as an interesting sound started to appear on one of the playbacks, but it ended just as quick. I thought I saw something out the corner of my eye, out the cottage window. I hit stop and turned around. Martin's small silhouette in the door frame, book in hand, looking down to his left. The ever-curious eyes on him.

Come on in, Martin. Join the party.

What are you two at?

I took some field recordings, Martin. The place we walked through the first night, remember, where we heard the crickets and the bird?

It was a rufous nightingale.

You caught us, Martin, Kate said as she walked out by him towards the kitchen. Red-handed, she shouted back.

Martin went over and sat on the floor by the open window, still looking at the ground. I placed a picnic blanket underneath him and Kate arrived back in with supplies. A carton of juice each and a selection of biscuits. We sat either side of him on the ground as we ate. Martin bit into one of the fig rolls and then stopped chewing a moment, his head tilted off to one side to study the way the crumbs fell and arranged themselves on the blanket. He finished his biscuit and drank his juice and then walked over to the screen and looked at the waves. He grabbed the jog-wheel and turned it many rotations to the left, minus 700 per cent slower than the original recording. With the mouse he selected the drop-down menu for the master output, rerouting the audio from the headphones to the monitors, like I showed him. He hit the spacebar and sat back down between us.

It was like these frozen tones then came out of the speakers, but only in terms of speed. The sounds themselves were warm. The cricket's chirps resembled giant warbling monks. The bird sounded like a Mongolian throat singer, a raspy ultra-low bass solo that weaved in and out of the cricket monks. But above all this came a female chant, and Martin looked towards the window and nodded to himself and closed his eyes. His face calm, just like any other child's face.

This new voice I couldn't account for in my audio editor. Its pitch and tone and rhythm had no visual wave like the rest of the sounds. It had just appeared, maybe as an excitatory sum of all the other parts, or possibly as a feedback loop from the extreme pitching-down process. A glitch, perhaps. But as much as I tried to, I didn't buy my own engineering rationale. This voice didn't sound like feedback, like some explainable audio accident. It came at us like a forgotten aria. A phantom bel canto trapped in the air that we'd unknowingly set free with our machines.

Martin started to rock back and forth. Kate rose to her feet. With her arms out wide, she began to spiral around the two of us, around the room. I closed my eyes and did a slow head-bang to Martin's song.

My father didn't speak those last few weeks of his life. For a man who was such a great talker, I'm having trouble swallowing this. Surely there were things he wanted to get off his chest before he went. Things he would have liked to say. I think about him all the more now, the older Martin gets. I try to remember how he was with me when I was Martin's age. I think about how Martin will be at my age. I can picture him as an adult, as a beautiful young man. Still lost in his world of books. But I see no wedding. No children by his side. I'm terrified of dying.

SHANDEEKA

Son

You wouldn't sing certain songs in the home house unless someone was holding your hand. Someone close to you and to the song. My father's father would always tend him as he found his way through the big songs. Their thick country fingers interlocked. And you'd know he was no longer in the room when he sang, my father. The good sean-nós singers are like that. They don't sing the songs so much as become them, anchored to the present by the held hand. But the anchor never worked on my father.

Mother

Her grandson pushes that new contraption of his close to her mouth and says, Do it again, Nana.

He presses a red button on the screen. When she sings she sees wave-like shapes rise and fall before her. That's you, the boy says, before his tongue pushes out from the inside of his cheek and he goes tapping buttons that appear and disappear again. Pulling things left and right. Twisting knobs that were seconds later buttons that were seconds later knobs. The light from the screen ghosting over his face.

They're like the waves we saw in Salthill last summer, Nana, but these ones are made of your sounds. That's why they're called sound waves.

She never considered the sounds that came from her voice to be waves, yet it makes complete sense. Waves move you, clean you, but can pull you under if you let them.

She gives him another one and he plays it back for her. There's a sea of low and smooth waves where the song begins and she gets how that is so – her rendition of 'Teddy O'Neill' always starts quiet, low in tone. The high and fat waves are where her voice hit its fullness. The red waves are where she lifted it, as she used always do, for the penultimate verse. The boy's fingers as busy now as she'd ever seen them – Just tidying things up a bit, Nana. It's a pity you wouldn't tidy your room that well, she says back, but she likes watching him work the sound. She loves seeing her song etch itself across the screen. A video taken of just her voice.

That album cover on the kitchen wall keeps catching her. Shandeeka's first LP, *Alight*. The photo taken close to a lake – was it Multyfarnham? Glasson? Her on a little wooden stool in the lime-green miniskirt. The Star McDonagh and Packie, God rest him, either side with their instruments. The wild hairdos. She's barely glanced at it for months but these last few weeks – it's the Star. There's almost a glow around him in that picture. An exact age she couldn't put on herself, but she was young. The only part she could still lay claim to would be the eyes. The eyes never seem to change.

The young lad is thorough at least – she likes that about him. We'll go again from the top, Nana. See where we can improve it. Go on so, she says back.

He hits play and the voice is good and clear. No messing about. A dull, honest recording sang straight into the hearth wall, stood on a thick rug. The tone of her voice crisp, compared to, say, the voice you'd envision comes out of the person who looks back at her every morning from the bathroom mirror. That potters quietly for the most part around her kitchen and living room and garden. The older she gets the quieter she gets until someone coaxes her to sing. And only within the singing of one does she remember how all her power still lies in song. Songs that will never age nor sicken nor lose a morsel of their strength. Songs that will outlive her and all belonging to her. They'll definitely outlive that yoke in her grandson's hand, her own son having paid silly money for it – twice the price of the Wren Anglo she had recommended for the boy down in McNeill's. A nice light concertina, perfect for the young lad to get going.

It's after maxing out again, Nana, and he points to those waves with the reddened tips.

Choppy waters, young man. There's choppy waters in 'Teddy O'Neill'.

She gives him it once more. When she sings the last, *But all I could answer was Teddy O'Neill*, the boy performs a whole go of well-timed button pushes. Her own voice sounds from the speaker in the corner of the kitchen. A speaker which is somehow connected to the phone in the boy's hands, even though no wire joins the two. He swears the song will be his long-term ringtone – he'll never change it. She nods the way someone would nod if they knew what a ringtone was, but tells him this: *Long-term*, that's a dangerous word for a small mouth. Live what you can for now and make no declarations about what you'll be thinking or doing tomorrow. You're better off knowing that now instead of waiting years to find it out.

Father

There were always songs I wanted, songs I had to have. The first time I went at 'Anach Cuain' in Uncle Seosamh's house, I got shot down midway through the first verse. A boy has no business there. But I didn't agree. Twelve or no twelve, I told them, I sing it as good as any of yee.

The explanation I was given by Seosamh, God be good to him, I failed to get my head around for the longest of times. Within sean-nós – he said in that voice that could have held any lecture hall in the country – within the lengthy nasal droned contours of songs, is buried a secret language. It is this language that needs excavating by the singer before it can be heard by the listener. The timbre of the voice a translator.

I have the right shape to my mouth, I said back. I have the ornamentation down to a tee. I might lack a bit of bottom end but that'll come, as everyone keeps telling me. I sing that song as good as you, and I half shaped up to him as I spoke.

Seosamh placed his right hand on my crown, leaving it sit there, gripped tight, like he was considering squashing his response into me. He reeked of smoke and turpentine. I steadied myself, focusing on the open fire. He told me that song was not mine yet, and he squeezed his fingers tighter again before flinging me back into his armchair.

And you'll never try that in my house again, not until you're ready. And every witness in this room could be dead and gone by that time.

How will I know, so, when I'm ready?

Seosamh shot a headful of air from his nostrils, no different to how a bull would if something unwanted approached, his voice as low and full as I'd ever heard it.

You'll fucken know when you know, lad. And there will be no doubt in your mind nor anyone that hears you that you're ready, because it won't be something that can be kept in. And it's not cadence of voice nor lilt nor breath nor shape of mouth nor fucken ornamentation what readies you for the big songs. I could teach the dog to ornament if I wanted, but there's much more going on under the hood when it comes to the sean-nós, *the old style*, as they call it. And why? Why is it called *the old style*? It's called so because if you haven't yet opened up the old wounds within yourself, wounds upon which these songs were built, then your performance of that song will bested by the dog's bark every time, as one will be as empty as the other.

Mother

When the technician wrote off her old Stanley 8, her son bought her the new back-boiler stove. The Stanley had four hot plates, the stove only one, but she knows his heart is in the right place. She opens its big glass door and wipes away the black smudge from last night's fire. The boy falls in behind her, clawing hot coals to the front with the hoe. She tongs the bigger ones that are still embering. They stack paper, thin timber cuts and fresh coals on top. An agreement is reached – even after everything is shaken down, there's enough room below for another night's ash.

When all is set, the boy reaches down to the bottom of the fuel box and pulls up the bellows and goes to hand it to her, smirking. Use that to light it, Nana.

I'd fart stronger than that thing. Now put it back in its wrapper and hold my hand.

Crouched down, she blows on last night's embers. The boy cheers when he sees the new flames and she finds it hard to keep in the smile as he helps straighten her up. Standing beside each other with their hands still joined, they look in. The stove's young flame. It's as good an entertainment as any.

She adjusts the air vents and dampers. The boy goes to the hot press and clambers up on top of the stool and pulls the red lever down. She knows from the quietness that comes on him when he walks back over and just stands beside the fire – there's questions lining up in his head. His father was no different.

Where did you learn to sing, Nana?

Something draws her gaze among the trees in the woods down the back. The feeling that someone is about to walk in the door, the phone is about to ring. An unspoken signal from the immediate future that often comes to her, a thing common to everyone, she supposes, although she's never asked. She waits. No door opens. No phone rings. Just a single pulse of light beyond the first few rows of trees. As strong as a lighthouse beacon but from the middle of the woods, low to the ground. Like the lighthouse is sunken. Has she not seen something similar before? She would convince herself that it was the eyes playing up, yet all every optician ever told her was that she could see around corners. There's forestry men doing work down there, that must be it, but she's not overly convinced. She knows a sign when she sees one.

Piloting his father's hand-me-down 1966 Morris Minor van, the Star McDonagh swung into her parents' yard to pick her up for Shandeeka's first gig. The left headlight missing so long the van was known locally as Cyclops. And the beam from Cyclops filled her with an energy that's never fully faded. That he may come straight through that sitting-room window, she said to the empty space around her as he drove up the driveway.

The Star's long bushy hair. He only starting to grow the beard around then. How exotic he could sometimes look playing his bouzouki. Packie McDonagh's double bass filling every room they gigged. The way the Star could work a slide guitar, even a harmonium on the odd song. His handwork was magnificent. Her sean-nós-shaped voice knitting itself in and out of his 3/4 rhythms.

The first spotlight of the national tour hit her in the Dean Crowe Hall in Athlone Town, 1969. She'd found her place. With the eyes closed she sang Pentangle's 'Light Flight', the Pecker Dunne's 'Sullivan's John'. For the last verse of 'As I roved out', she turned and sang straight at the Star. He harmonized in a soft baritone. It wasn't planned, but it became part of the act. *When broken shells make Christmas bells, we might well get married.*

They played their own material after the break. It got the biggest reaction of the night. Her voice embellished in thick double bass and electrified with sharp hits off the Star's bouzouki. They finished off with a set of reels and the encore was a slow air, over which she improvised a lilt.

A scout from Island Records approached them afterwards. The Star went outside with him for a cigarette. At the back of the balcony she placed her hand on the large bulb of the spotlight, a burning heat still coming off it.

Her own voice sings in the room now beside her. The young man using his two hands to bring the rectangular phone to his ear. Hi, Dad. The singing stops and she goes back looking at the woods. Wondering ever wondering, had she seen anything down there at all. Thinking – when the boy finishes talking to his father, she'll answer his question. It was in the light where she learned how to sing.

Son

My father lived so much in the world of song that when he sat at the dinner table with us, you'd see from his eyes he was elsewhere. He left one morning just after dawn. He couldn't bring himself to lie down beside my mother – the electricity that lingered in his body and mind after a gig he didn't want to end. So he married the songs instead and never left them. Standing at my nursery door, he saw a baby in the cot and knew that it was the son of the man who stood in that doorway. But another part of him was already out in the middle of the road with a suitcase waiting for the lift to the ferry, looking in on himself and the baby and the sleeping wife. The silhouette of our terraced house in the small hours. He still claims he never wanted to leave us – he just had to go and get the songs.

I told him to go fuck himself when he told me that yarn. But I do find myself more and more looking back on the black-and-white footage of him performing in those days in London. And when I watch and hear him sing, I start to understand why he left. I forgive him each time I listen, briefly.

The BBC had cameras in Les Cousins music club on Greek Street in Soho the night my father was called up to sing. In the 'Anach Cuain' video, a Rasta woman held his hand. She seemed competent enough and guided him along, standing in front of him but just off to the side, him perched on a high stool, one foot on the rest, the other long leg stretched off to his left. Their brown and white hands making small synchronous movements. Circling around, back and forth. The odd jolt throwing both hands off before they settled again into those small movements. It was impossible to say which hand was guiding which, or whether my father's explanation had some merit – that it was the song itself what guided things.

Long-haired teens from inner city London, an old Black man in a straw hat, flower-power heads, straitlaced-looking folk in suits, all stared at my father as he sang. Each one of them wearing the same face. They wouldn't have had a word of Irish between them, but they all understood what was being sung. 'Anach Cuain' is a lament, a class of a requiem – as my mother describes it – for a village of people whose boat failed them off the Galway shore. And my father sang it like he was loss himself, everyone recognizing its true sound once they heard it. He sang it in a way no one had yet sang in Les Cousins. He sang it in a way no one had yet sang 'Anach Cuain'.

John Renbourn and Burt Jansch watched from the bar. Paul Simon performed the following week and people told him about my father. I couldn't care less who was there, I told him when he started to drop names. I'm sorry, he said. I know, I know you don't care about that stuff, but I had to go. I wouldn't have survived if I didn't.

Mother

Her grandson calls out. The young man is hungry. That thing she was going to say to him is gone. Something about the stove or trumpets. It's gone. If it's important it'll come back.

The woods – that was nothing. There's always been a tendency to read too much into light. Keep it to herself would be the best thing. Sheila Gannon went around saying what she was seeing and they had her in the Stella Maris before the end of the month. She'll heat up two hot cross buns for herself and the boy.

He smiles when he sees the buns come out of the bread bin and goes back about his phone business. Ambidextrous his thumbs. The sound of his small fingers rapping off glass. Movement fast and steady. A nice flow of low beeping sounds. If they'd bought you that concertina, you'd be Fleadh Cheoil material by now. You could accompany me here beside the fire. We could tour. I have contacts, you know. And God knows you have the genes, God bless us all.

I'm not allowed, he says without looking up. Daddy says listening and recording is OK, but playing music is dangerous. He says that's how he lost his daddy. Is that true, Nana?

You wouldn't know what's true these days. Every time I look back something else has changed.

Grandad gave me a whistle, Nana, when we visited him last year. It was a Kerry. Daddy got drunk when he came home and threw it in the bin. Did Matt Molloy play a Kerry?

By the time she responds the boy is gone. His little body and busy thumbs haven't budged, but his mind is off gallivanting inside that black screen. He wouldn't hear a meg of what she said from now on. The speed of them fingers – concertina player if she ever saw one.

Maybe her son was right. Or maybe himself over the water was right to have bought the boy a whistle. What he might look like now. Was it even his fault? If she were him and he her, she might well have left herself. She knows the future is set in stone, but the past reshapes itself daily depending on how she holds it up for inspection. How she listens to it. She'll tend the buns, that'd be the best thing to do. The smell will bring him back.

She kneels down on a kitchen towel and looks in. The oven's red element warms her forehead. She closes her eyes and takes the heat. Opens them when she feels a burn and carefully places the buns on the tray and closes the oven. She pulls herself back to her feet and walks to the conservatory to take a quick rest on the wicker chair, looking down on the back fields and the woods.

Father

I got the visit last year. Lucky enough they didn't bring the talking shoes – I had no words for them neither. Me and Joe, we would have the odd conversation on the phone. Some bad but some fairly good. He opens up some nights when he has a few pints in him. Things is just different though, faced off in a small room.

Ini left us to it after they arrived and closed the kitchen door to start on the grub. I sat in my armchair and looked at the boy. The boy looked at the place where I suppose he'd expect a television to be. Joe had the two hands on the knees like an aeroplane was about to take off.

I threw the boy up on my lap and hummed him 'Aililiú na Gamhna'. He grabbed my thumbs and held them as I went through it. Then the silence was there. Ini! Can you stick that aul sound system on for us? Matt Molloy, I told her when she came back in. 'The Humours Of Ballyloughlin'.

I tapped my foot to the jig and the boy tapped his. He closed the eyes and moved the head side to side to Matt's flute playing. He has it, you know, I told Joe. That boy of yours, you'd know by the hands and the feet. He knows how to listen. Wouldn't you know, Ini? I shouted back in to her. Joe kept it quiet, of course. Sitting there staring at his son on my lap, as if I might harm the boy.

I put him down and looked around but I couldn't see it. Ini! I don't know where I left that present.

She came back in again and placed the long thin leather pouch into the young lad's hands. It's a Kerry, I told Joe, even though the name was etched into the pouch. A low D. He'll get a lifetime out of it if he minds it. It'll start tune his ear. Just leave him play with it like any other toy and it'll soon be fairly clear that the boy has it. He could be the next Matt Molloy.

Joe told the boy leave the whistle in the case for now. Ini went to walk away into the kitchen and I asked her how long it'd be. It's ready when it's ready, she said. Leave the door open, I asked her, but she closed it behind her. She doesn't like the smells spreading, I explained, but more to the room itself than anyone in it.

The quiet came back as quick as it had left. The flat shrinking in around me. Everyone and everything was too close. I put the boy on my lap again and closed the eyes. I gave him 'The Rocks of Bawn'.

Ini brought out the rice and peas and chicken jerky and the young lad pushed the food around the plate. Ini asked Joe: Why ya come see your father if you're not gonna talk to the man?

It was the young lad wanted to come, he said. He wanted to see the set-up. I'll never deny him seeing his grandfather.

Gwan Joe, she told him. And I loved when she revved up. Her patois coming through more than the London accent. She has great fire in her.

Blaming the boy, she said, like a boy do himself. Talk if ya come, man. Stay away if ya quiet. Ask the man how he been at least. He been sick this past while.

I knew well Joe wouldn't reply. He was bulling over the whistle. In fairness, he'd asked me not to buy any more instruments. I don't want to see the family craft die out with me, I told him, but I might as well have been telling the wall. It was me gave him that face anyways. The one you'd pull at a dinner table you felt you didn't belong at. Resenting everyone for making you be there in the first place.

It's not a bother, Ini, I told her. He wanted me to see the young lad is all. Fair play to them for making the travel.

Ini saw them to the door before the plates were cleared off the table. Joe didn't say goodbye as he walked out.

Bring ya chat next time, Joe. We be here.

Thanks for the food, Ini, he said back. The young lad gave me a hug. Examining the leather pouch as he walked away.

Ini packed up a few things that evening and headed for her sister Nancy's house. She knows well when I need to be left alone, God bless her mind.

Mother

The clouds break and wedges of light cut down through the panelled glass above her. The slow gait of the boy walking up behind. He's quiet. He has questions. Without opening the eyes she says, Go on.

Nana, you never answered me about the circular breathing. What? I asked you could they hold the notes forever, the trumpet players. You didn't. I did, Nana.

She licks the corner of her apron and wipes away a milk stain from above his lip. He winces, no different to his father at that age, although she's a lot gentler with the boy. She's not proud of the way she treated her own the first few years. She had no one else to take it out on.

The record company had invested a lot of money in them – that was the spiel she got off the agent. She more or less owed it to them to do the US tour. The Carnegie Hall gig. The agent had a doctor lined up – they'd done it many times before so there was nothing to worry about. But she told the agent she'd be having the baby. She told the Star to find a replacement for her – the girl he ended up marrying.

But if she'd gone herself. If she didn't duck away the night the Star tried kiss her and they both promised to others at the time. I don't give a fuck about any of it, the Star told her. Not the music, the girlfriend, the tours. But she walked away and went back in and sat beside her own man in the singer's circle.

The boy tugs on her apron: Can they hold a tone forever or not, the trumpeters? Can you do it, Nana – the circular breathing? If you could, you could hold a note forever, could you not?

The clouds coagulate and the conservatory darkens around her. She turns to answer the boy but he's nowhere to be seen. Down the back field and right in the middle of the forest, she sees the pulse of light. It sweeps across the length of the woods like a giant's torch.

Son

I find him alone in a kitchen full of black smoke. The French doors in the conservatory wide open. I think she went down to the woods, he tells me. She forgot to put on her wellies. Why would she walk out the door without putting her wellies on?

Barefoot behind a tree in the middle of the woods, peeking out at something up ahead, she looks back and puts her index finger to her lips to *sssh* us quiet. She points to a place in the centre of the woods. I walk up beside her and coax her away from the tree and tell her it's teatime. There's no workmen down there, she tells us as we link her back up to the house. I knew it all along. I'm not blind. Why didn't you put on your wellies, Nana? What? Your feet, Nana. They're soaking.

I arrange a few days off work and hang around the house to keep an eye on her. More and more I come across her looking down towards the woods. She speaks less each day. The fire doesn't get lit until I do it and the kitchen seems like someone else's without the smell of her baking. We make a deal – she can spend the mornings in her wicker chair just outside the conservatory doors once she comes inside in the evening. She insists on being barefoot so we wrap her in blankets and leave one under her feet. The young lad has the iPhone on record standby all the time. It must be the first time she's ignored his request for a song. When she goes a full fortnight without singing, I know we're in trouble. Dr Tom comes and runs some tests and afterwards calls me out to the hallway and closes the door behind him.

Mother
The outlines of the trees begin to splinter away from the trees themselves. They sway in opposite directions. There is a separate woods, a shadow of

the one that has always been on display. She doesn't want to take her eyes away in case she misses the reveal.

Everything sharpens. All the minute changes that occur unnoticed every day in the backyard. She can sense trails of ants walk by before she sees them. Grass growing in real time. How has she never noticed the way her gardens and the woods react to a badly needed shower of rain? Or to a badly needed blast of sunlight? Silent applause is what it's like. It's as moving a song as she's heard.

To sit long enough and see the same sleeping flowers awake, unfurl, grow, shine and wither. There's no panic in anything at all. There's little to no interest in food but she lets them stuff the necessary into her so that afterwards they'll leave her be. If there is a change in the woods, the grass, the flowers, she turns and keeps whoever is there up to date.

Son

She can barely keep herself fully upright in the chair. I came across her slumped over to the side one morning after her elevenses. She hadn't even noticed herself going down. The face on her like she was watching an interesting film on the concrete path beneath her chair. Her head at an awful angle.

Myself and the young lad set up camp in the spare room. I arrange to work remotely, half-converting the living room into an office. We find her slumped and dozing, day in, day out. When I find her sound asleep today, I lift her from her wicker chair and carry her upstairs and place her on her bed.

We bring as many of the house plants up as will fit in the room. The two bonsai trees on each locker and the two buddha tea-light holders in front. At night she watches the miniature trees. The candles throw shadows onto the window wall. The bonsai trees look enormous over there, the boy's eyes bulging as he whispers.

Mother
Afternoon light is distinctive and full and gets everywhere. The medication is strong. The blur. She nudges the odd pill under her tongue. Later she buries them down into the bonsai's soil.

She wakes and sees a set of flashes rise from the woods. It's just about possible to make out the tips of the trees down there. There's a pattern to the flashing, some class of a message.

Son
The boy insists on bringing the bellows up to her. It always works, he tells me. She'll come down and get the fire going once she sees this thing is out.

He stands beside the bed and stares at her, muttering something about Louis Armstrong. He looks down again at the bellows. That can be your job now, I tell him. You'll get the hang of how to use it. But he erupts beside the bed. We don't use the bellows, he says. Nana blows on the fire and it comes on and I put this thing back in its wrapper where it belongs. Don't I, Nana?

The priest calls by every week, then every other day, then every morning. Sometimes twice a day. She surely knows herself by now. The boy asks the priest did he ever hear of circular breathing. We make him more tea before he leaves, walk him out to the car and watch him drive off.

Dad? Yeh. Why are we giving her all the pills? To kill the pain. Why? Because I don't want Nana to be in pain. But they're making her sleep all the time. That's good, son – she needs rest.

Dad? Yeh. Are we killing her? What? Nana said before that they killed Packie McDonagh with the tablets. The drink killed Packie McDonagh, son – the tablets were for the pain.

Dad? Yeh. Can we go down to the woods?

We stand among the trees where we found her. Himself looking around like a little detective. What do you think she saw down here, Dad? I don't know – what do you think she saw?

He kneels down and studies a small mound of blackened twigs on the forest floor.

Mother

Visitors come and go. Some of them she recognizes, some of them she doesn't want to see. Some she's never seen before.

The house heats up. Cools down. The blankets. Even two becomes too much. Their weight is cutting straight through her. Small fibres press into her raw flesh like knives. Her son and the young man land in with a contraption. It lifts the sheets and blankets an inch or two from her skin. She can breathe again.

Music comes from the corner. When she is turned in the bed she sees her turntable and LPs. Nick Drake is playing. The Bothy Band. Joe Heaney. Ravi Shankar. The boy comes up and sits beside her and hits the red button on his contraption and starts to talk. It's like he's learned a new language – she can't make out anything he says. The boy's father carries him away and his strong cries don't affect her.

Ravi's sitar strings and ragas start to lure her from the room. She sits up and looks around, looks back down at herself in the bed. Down at the back fields and the woods. The shadows of the trees sway wildly, but the trees themselves don't move.

Son

I wake around 2 a.m. and I hear her singing 'Teddy O'Neill'. As good as she ever sang it. I turn on the lamp and the young lad has the Bluetooth speaker in his arms, looking at the waves work across the screen.

He shakes me at 4 a.m. Come on, she's awake.

He likes to hold the straw up to her lips when she makes the thirst sound. With the tongue pushing out his cheek, he wipes the spittle from her chin as though she were made of crystal.

She moves her head up and down and makes a whining noise – It's the bedsores sound, Dad.

We turn her over and take off the dressings. The big one over her right hip is the worst. What do you call the rocks that fall from the sky sometimes? Asteroids. What's the hole they make? Craters. Isn't it like a little asteroid has smashed into Nana? All red raw and black around the edge. Don't say that. Why not? It's your nana. It's not nice – she's sick. But that's what it's like, he says again. Why don't you go down and make me a cup of tea and I'll do this? He shakes the head. I give him the tub and he doesn't flinch in applying the cool gel with his thumb around the edges of the sore. I can barely look straight at it myself. He's right. It is just like a fresh crater, still burning. We put on the dressing and cover it up with a foam pad. I pull the covers up over the blanket lifter.

What's the smell, Dad? It's just the smell that happens when you're ill. Will grandad get the bedsores as well? I don't know. Will we put the gel on him? No. Ini will.

Mother

By the type of darkness in the room, it's close to midnight. She can sense someone before she opens the eyes. In the chair beside the bed is an old man. Only when he smiles does he become the Star McDonagh. As beautiful a man as she knew he would be when elderly. The smell of the flowers from the Dean Crowe Hall the night they got signed. The Star's aftershave the night he tried kiss her. He doesn't speak at her bedside. He never needed to talk to make her feel good. He places his hand inside hers. She nods at him and he nods back. He looks around at the record player. When he turns he sings, but in a whisper, repeating the lines she's always loved, the ones they always duetted – *Frosty weather, snowy weather, when the wind blows, we all blow together. Frosty weather, snowy weather, when the wind blows sure we'll all go together.*

She can hear slow, heavy footsteps on the stairs.

Light entering the room changes how she feels. Her voice, the words, are gone. She listens to her own steady wheeze until it becomes part of the room. It wasn't a dream nor a vision – the Star McDonagh really was here. He left Liam Clancy's voice. Joe Heaney. Joan Baez. If in the next life the chance comes again. If the gurus are right. She'll marry the Star and never leave him.

Son

It's hard to say if she's asleep or awake – her eyes never fully close. Her face has an expression like she's listening to something, even when there's total silence.

She has new sounds for pain and for dry mouth, sounds for want of more music and for turn the music off. She has other sounds I can't decipher. We take turns listening to her, changing her dressings, changing the records. We haven't closed the curtains since she came upstairs.

Mother

There are many people standing around her bed. Smiling, crying. She can hear what sounds like a prayer but it could be a song. Inside herself she is completely alone.

The sun comes up over the trees and thousands of dust particles float in the air between her and the window. She's been sleeping in invisible snow all her life. The bonsai trees, the Star's lilies, her records, her hair. Everything must be layered in the stuff. It makes the record crackle more than ever. Is that

Emmylou? Dolores Keane? Margaret Barry? Their voice swirls the dust. She dozes as the light fully fills the room.

Son

This morning she made convulsive, pig-like grunts, and her eyes opened very wide and she pushed her chest up in the bed like she was being electrocuted. An hour later her breath went quiet. She's gone, someone said. She's gone, Joe.

I didn't handle it great. I don't know what came over me, but I started shouting for her to come back. The young lad beside me in an awful way, but she took a massive gulp of air and the wheezing started again.

I'll have to do better when she does go – she wouldn't want that sort of pandemonium in the room. The priest and all there. I brought the young lad for a spin to the shops afterwards to clear the heads. He stayed quiet until we got out onto the main road.

Dad? Yeh. Why is Nana making them new sounds? I don't know. You thought she was dead, didn't you? I suppose I did, yeh. She's not dead though is she? She's not, no.

Dad? Yeh. Can I have a trumpet? No, you can't.

Dad? Yeh. Can we get hot cross buns? We can, yeh.

DID YOU EVER HEAR OF ALFONSO, THE YOUNG KING OF SPAIN?

My father. Born Irish. Changed allegiance and moved to Spain. Swore an oath and took the soup.

My father. Possessor of a Spanish passport, and soon to be the possessor of a Spanish tombstone, will never come home – was he ever home? Do those photos on the mantelpiece not prove it – that he loved his wife and child?

My father was queer, queer all along. Even in those photos. I don't hate him for his queerness. The polar opposite. I hate him for hiding it. I hate him for not being real until it was too late and I hate the shameful way he left and I hate the thoughts that visitors now have when they come into our home and glance at the old photos on the mantelpiece. I can hear their thoughts – I am not deaf.

Gloria calls. I stop packing. She tells me I am at Stage 1: Denial.

Gloria girl, I'm in no denial. There's no denying dead things, it's binary on or off, alive or dead, everyone is guaranteed to be in one of these states at all times, and my father is in the latter at the moment. And lest we forget, he was the one who was in denial.

I'm here if you need me girl, she says.

I'm here if *you* need me, I say.

And you should cut back on the Q word, she tells me. It's still derogatory in some circles.

Queer is *not* derogatory girl.

Still is to some people.

Gloria, stop. My friend Two. You know Two?

Yeh.

They took Queer Theory in Maynooth.

Sure you can study anything in Maynooth.

Queer's been taken back girl. Reclaimed – joy, pride, defiance, that's what it means now.

Meanings don't change for everyone overnight, babe.

I have a queer father, Gloria. A queer friend. I am way overqualified for this conversation.

Just not everyone is OK with it yet, that's all I'm saying. Please, just go pack.

I'm jumping online, Gloria.

Don't.

I'm online. Cambridge dictionary. Queer – examples of use:

Growing up, I knew in my heart I was queer.

I find myself infuriated by this attitude of shame and guilt, as do many other queer men.

Derek Jarman was an English pioneer in queer cinema.

The queer community is inclusive and incorporates all these identities.

Stop. I surrender.

Of course you surrender.

Now go about your business and get to the airport.

And get it over with, I add.

Call me when you get there.

I will.

Love and alignment.

Love and alignment.

I make the airport in good time. Time enough to squeeze in a mojito. The barman serves me as if nothing has happened. He looks like he could play sport instead of having to think his way through life. I consider throwing my mojito across the bar at him, but he looks too good, as does the drink. I sip. I look at photos of my father on my phone. A picture of us outside the squash courts at O'Connor Park. The day he anchored his tug-of-war team to gold. Pictures of us in agricultural co-ops and hardwares and building concrete walls.

A message comes in from Gloria. She's changed her profile to me and her looking happy on a night out. Full armour, 75 per cent flesh on show. I ask Barman what he thinks. Beautiful ladies, he says. I find Gloria attractive too, I tell him. We have kissed drunk, but I am predominantly interested in young men. Oh right, he says. Most of my friends, apart from Gloria and Two, are young men. Two? What kind of a name is that? I find a picture of Two. Barman's eyebrows lower as he looks at the picture. Two's parents assigned them a binary gender when they were born but they feel more comfortable not pinned to a point on the gender spectrum – are you OK with that? Barman nods, looks around, finds some patches of bar to wipe down a little away from me.

We stand by Two, I raise my voice. We stand by their strength to come out and just say it. To just fucking say it. Barman moves back a bit and says in a low, political voice, I have to go and serve someone. I grab his arm. They took the name Two after we all watched Dustin Hoffman's classic *Little Big Man* – Arthur Penn, 1970 – upon Two's suggestion, when they decided enough was enough. The character Little Horse, played by Robert Little Star, was a Native American two-spirit person. I recommend everyone and their mother to watch that movie.

Barman tugs his arm free and slips away. Tells me he'll be back in a minute. I feel I'm being incinerated from the belly out.

I find the picture of my father drinking a pint out the back of Joe Lee's Bar and me on his lap. It does me no good. Mammy beside him with her hand on his thigh and a delicate smile on her face. She's a cleaner in that photo, Mammy. A good one at that. A beautiful one. But the shaking starts and the Parkinson's retires her from her work, her activities, her life, aged way too young. I sip a little more. To my father, I declare loud enough for Barman and his new customer to hear. Born on a cold little island, born to flesh, soon to be planted alone in hot Spanish soil, ashes in a can. A drop of whiskey on his grave if he's lucky. Hated by his only daughter. Well done, Father, well done. Hip hip!

I floor my mojito and raise my glass for more – this one's not working.

Who am I to call you out? I am your daughter, that's who. Always a good excuse. I am an only child to boot and that brings its own complications. I am fatherless since long before you died. I am now fearless of what I say. I am full of rage, the same rage you stuffed into my eyes when I was a little girl. And I like the rage. So thanks for that but it does tend to land me in unusual situations. I could shake you, Father. I could shake you so that you come back to life, so that I may strangle you to death again. That's who I am to call you out.

I've been writing notes like this since my father died. Then I torch them. It's known as the letter-burn ritual. Write down what you want forgiven, forgotten, good riddance to. I can't yet speak of the long-term benefits, but I do feel fractionally lighter after each burn.

I went to the county library yesterday morning and asked to see the *Offaly Independent* archives, early noughties. I was looking for the day my father got called out at an Offaly senior county football final. I find it – September 2002. Tullamore versus Gracefield, O'Connor Park. I squint into the archive photos on the screen but I can't zoom in enough

to see us. I know we are there. I know Jimmy
Roundbale Delaney is there.

Midway through the half-time interval, Jimmy
Roundbale Delaney calls my father a *faggot*
and a *poofter*. My six-year-old mind has no idea
what a *faggot* or a *poofter* is, but by the way the
Roundbale's face scrunches up when he says the
words, I know they're not good. Jimmy Roundbale
is not from either club. He shows allegiance to no
team in the county but goes to each match. Heckles
every referee. He has sat out many lengthy bans
but still returns. My father and myself, we are The
More. We are The Faithful.

My father gets verbally abused in front of The
Faithful. In front of his only daughter, and he does
something about it. He grabs Jimmy Roundbale
by his floppy man tits and drags him to the aisle.
Batters him against the concrete steps. Batters him
with his fists. It's the bunched fists that keep the
shame locked up, Two tells me out of nowhere last
week. And my father's fists, they get the job done.
They shut Jimmy Roundbale up.

It was not a pretty sight, but the Roundbale
was well padded and he survived. This is my first
recorded memory. Verified in print by the *Offaly
Independent* archives. The journalist reported that
Tullamore *clinched the game at the death with a
beautiful point from just inside the 45. Outside of*

the left boot. There is no mention of the assault. Jimmy Roundbale probably got patched up by the Order of Malta outside O'Connor Park. Too proud to press any charges. And my father, since September 2002, has been called a *faggot* and a *poofter* by absolutely no one.

Outside a hospital called Ramón y Cajal, blue skies, I can see Madrid's mountains in the distance. I have explained umpteen times to my mother that there are ancient laws in Spain that govern the dead. Some old king made it so that no one who said they belonged to the place could be buried outside it. The Spanish are alright but they have big ideas about themselves. My father had given up his right to go home when he swapped the Irish for the continental passport. He would be cremated and entombed here. The sooner the better.

The Spanish don't fuck about with the dead, Mammy.

I don't get it, love, and mind your language, please.

There's not much to get. They brought in the law centuries ago and then himself arrives from Ireland and swears an oath when he gets here and the rest is history.

He's not a *himself*, love, he's your father.

He changed nationalities, Mother dear. He took the fucken soup.

Stop it, love. Just stop it.

Sorry Mammy, sorry. I didn't mean it. You know what I'm like in the sun. I have to go, the doctor's about to bring me in.

In where?

Call me in ten, Mammy.

OK, love.

Standing over my father in the morgue, I lay my hand on his cold forehead, just to make sure. But my hand won't lift away. My thumb brushes his hair back. He's grown his beard again. When I would go in to wake him on Sundays to go swimming, he used to pretend he was still asleep for ages before opening his eyes. I wait for him to open his eyes now. Gloria calls, I walk outside.

You are repressing your love for him. Grief is like this. It comes in stages. I feel you have now moved from Stage 1, Denial, to Stage 2, Anger. I feel you are in the anger stage now, babe.

Gloria girl, you're my best friend in the world. You are the crème de la fucking crème, but do not tell me what I am feeling about my dead father.

Gloria is cool with my response. We have always been straight with each other. Kept each other in check through nursery/primary/secondary/third level. She is me and I am her. Love and alignment will prevail. But I can't examine myself now. The inner judge can go fuck herself for a day or two. I want Spanish beer. I want cheap Spanish tobacco. I want to grope a young brown-skinned man with perfect white teeth. I want to surgically remove the portion of my mind labelled *father stuff*, through hedonistic practices alone if possible.

I smoke and gaze at the mountains. Thoughts devour me. My father fathered one child. Stayed straight until that child finished university and his wife finally got her disability benefit and then he left for the continent to be with his fancy man. Stop, I tell myself out loud.

My father. Stop.

My father was never anywhere to be seen during Pride Week. He always went fishing on his own during the first week of July. Stop.

On one of the trips, we don't know which, he met his fancy man. Francisco. My father's man is called Francisco.

A Spaniard approaches and asks for *fuego* and makes a clicking motion with his thumb and he smiles and his smile settles me. I want to marry him, here and now. He is perfection. When asked, he tells me he is a cleaner and I tell him about

Mammy and we talk about the mountains. I veer the chat towards history, something I know about, my degree in Maynooth – History with a 2.1. My master's in Cultural Studies with a first, yada yada yada. I blow smoke cool as you like from the side of my mouth. His teeth are china white. I want to lick his biceps. I am well versed in the historical and we talk civil war. We talk Irish brigades. We talk Orwell and then he talks Lorca and now I am in over my head. I get desperate to impress. I get brave. I say the forbidden word. *Franco*. I say it again. Spanish boy coughs and lowers his voice and glances behind him.

Escuchame tía, the truth? These hospital, here, we stand at, we build after Franco die as no one want to go to other hospital close by where he die. You understand?

Sí sí, I say.

Franco, he build the other hospital for his son. Is there, close. Franco call it Hospital La Paz – the Hospital of Peace. Imagine, no. Franco and peace. But the thing is, for the days after he die, my grandmother she a nurse on the ward and my grandmother, *mi abuelita* –

Spanish boy stops talking. His granny washes through his eyes. He becomes even more perfect now that he has sadness in him.

He whispers, *Mi abuelita* was a *rojo*. You understand *rojo, tía*?

Sí sí.

He is telling that me she was a red. A rebel against Franco. I love his granny now too. I move nearer to him to hear the rest, so close that it would be classed as inappropriate in some cultures.

Mi abuelita, she worked on that floor where Franco they took him when he was sick, near the end, no. She bring him food. She clean his shit. When he lose the conscious, she whisper in his ear. She tell Franco where he was going to go when he go, no? And then she explain me these other thing. She say me that after Franco die, no one is able to enter that room for one month. Not his loyal soldiers. Not his family. Not even God.

The Spaniard's storytelling capabilities seal the deal. I picture my wedding dress as he types my number into his phone. I finish my business with the doctor and agree to come back tomorrow. At the train station, I await the Spaniard. I dream of cold beer. *Cerveza.* Cocktails. Cigarettes. Hotel sex. My chosen tools to extract my father from within.

You could been have been a local hero. You could have saved many other young men the pain. You were big and strong and well respected. You could have defended yourself. I would have defended you. I would have stood by you. I would have grown up with it and been used to it by the time I could swim. You could have bought the house next door and still brought me to school every day. You could have moved Francisco in. Mammy would have met someone else. She was so beautiful when she was young. She wouldn't be at home now on her own trying to steady herself enough to pour milk into her tea. Disability benefit does not have loving hands. It does not pour milk into your tea after you get Parkinson's. The people who love you are meant to do that.

I wake in my hotel room. Phone ringing. Missed calls from Mammy and Gloria. My head feels like someone else's. I rummage, without opening my eyes, in my handbag. I find the Solpadeine. I send thanks to whoever is responsible for the beautifully lenient codeine laws in Ireland. I drop two into a glass of water and the relief is quick. My phone rings again.

I want to come over, love.

I'm sorry Mammy, they're doing it today. I told you, they don't mess about here.

Can't they wait a few days?

You're going nowhere with your Michael Parkinson's Mam. And you know it.

I'm so sorry Mammy. I had a bit of a night last night, I don't know what I'm saying. Anyways, there's just no time. The undertakers never even shut here. It's just conveyor-belt stuff.

What about the wake, love?

No wakes Mammy. No dancing the corpses around the sitting room. No good china or egg-and-onion sandwiches. No decades and decades of the rosary. No whiskey whiskey whiskey.

OK, love. OK. I understand. This is not some sort of a joke, you know.

I'm sorry Mammy. Fuck. I'm just hanging from last night. Look, it will be dignified today. He'll get a good send-off. They have companies here who provide online services, you know – they can stream the whole thing.

They can what, love?

They can put it on the internet and you can watch it on your phone.

I watch *Coronation Street* on the phone, love. I watch *Emmerdale*. I don't watch your father's cremation on the phone. Have we no other options?

I walk to the *terraza* of the hotel room. The blue sky eases me into the seat. I decide to tell Mammy what the other option is and immediately regret it. She goes quiet.

It's OK Mammy. The doctor says it's not overly common but it is possible, they could do it, but obviously I said it wasn't for us.

Talk about déjà vu, love. I remember watching a documentary with your father. I don't know, it could have been ten years ago. *The Box* or *The Box Heart* or something it was called. They said that's what they used to do back in the day.

Back in what day?

When we were all poor and no one could afford to take a body back from America, they would send just the heart home by ship. They had a special lock-up on each boat. *The Heart Box*, that's what it was called.

Mammy. This is too weird.

It's where all the business gets done, you know. Our whole lives are kept in our hearts. Oh God, imagine we saw that together. I never thought –

I am not sitting on a plane with daddy's ticker in the overhead locker.

You need to listen to me now. You are going to do this for me. Not for your father, for me, please. I need something for the coffin.

I'm sorry, I can't.

You're thinking of yourself again. You think this is all about you and your feelings and your hurt. I'll be down there one day too, you know. I don't want to be alone. Do you understand what it's like to be alone all the time?

I hear the final whistle. I know it's all over.

I'll do it Mammy. Of course I will. I'm sorry. I'll ring them now and confirm it.

Gloria calls.

What happened?

I had a night.

Don't say?

I won't so.

What's happening?

I tell her about the letter-burning. She was the one who recommended the practice. Gloria likes to be kept updated on her recommendations.

Stage 3, she says.

What?

You've moved to Stage 3: Bargaining. It's all the modals you're using. Should, could haves, would haves. It's looking for excuses and ways things could have been different. I was literally just listening to a podcast about Stage 3. You are now at the bargaining stage of grief. You are doing super, babe.

Gloria girl, I just cannot.

Stay strong, babe.

I hang up.

The cleaner boy walks out from the *terraza* and hugs me from behind and pulls me back to bed. The codeine pulls the thoughts from my head. I show no resistance.

When I wake up I am a complete mess. The Spaniard asks what is wrong. Hay fever, I tell him. I have chronic hay fever. My phone rings. The hospital.

I await the doctor in an office beside the morgue. She walks in with a nurse who carries a white box. It is shiny, a velvet-coloured strip around its centre and a respectable-looking locking device. *Human remains, handle with care* written on it in many languages in large font. The doctor gives me the papers for customs. I sign. She explains everything then goes quiet as the nurse hands me the box. The doctor leaves with the papers.

I hold the box. Staring at it starts to weigh on me, like I want to lie down, so I sit it on my lap. I see myself sitting on his lap in O'Connor Park. Out the back of Joe Lee's. Pulling his beard.

The nurse seems a genuinely nice woman. She could easily be Mammy's age but she's on the ball. She takes Kleenex from a shelf and places them on the desk in front of me before I even start. When she puts her hand on my shoulder, I get worse. I know she's the type of woman that would be hard to bullshit, but autopilot kicks in and I give it a go. I put my emotion down to the hangover – they are known to bring out unexplained emotions. I also have hay fever, I say. She pushes the box of Kleenex even closer again and I take one and then another.

Eso es, hija. Eso es. Tómate tu tiempo.

She stands behind me and just rests her hands on my shoulders.

My father is now a heart inside a small box beside me on the bed in my hotel room. When I go to the toilet, I leave the door ajar so I can keep an eye on him.

My father rang me from Dublin airport three years ago. He did not tell me the truth. He just said that he was moving to Spain. I said, Fuck you Daddy, and I hung up. That was the last thing I said to him. Gloria likes to say that it's the fiery side of my character she loves the most. If that's the case, she must really adore me.

I come from a long line of fire. A great-granduncle a bare-knuckle boxer in Montreal in the late 1800s. An aunt a UFC cage fighter at bantamweight. A grandfather who still goes daily to the woods in Charleville Castle and buries his head in the ground and screams and roars himself empty. He claims it makes for longevity.

A Spanish phone number appears in a message in my inbox. From my mother.

Go on, love. Ring him. It's the right thing to do x.

A long procession through barren hot landscape. The parade leader holds a beating heart in the air. Sacrificially, it seems to me. People chant and bow as the procession passes. I run alongside. I am a young girl. Asking, Is that my daddy's heart? Is that Daddy? No one understands me. I cry. I flood the desert. Trees sprout instantaneously and one hooks me and I dangle in the air as the parade and its followers and the heart all get swept away by the floods. I hang onto the tree and am terrified to touch the water. I hang there waiting for you to come back and rescue me. But you don't come.

The knock knock pings me back into my hotel room. I scull my mini-bar G&T and pick my father up and walk over to the door. But I'm holding him like he's a present for someone so I put him under my arm.

Francisco, the man says to me when I open the door. He nods at me, waiting for a reply. And you must be –

Yes, yes, I tell him. It's me. Come in.

He is impressively structured. All his own hair. Streaky grey beard and eyes well bagged from the tears. He starts again when he meets me. I look like my father, apparently. That's genetics, Francisco. He awkwardly reaches down to hug me and I cobra myself away and place instead the box into his hands and I slip into the bathroom.

He calls after me – What is in the box?

On the way through the park, we pass the box back and forth. Francisco tells me they used to come here every evening, while my father could still walk.

Nice park.

It used to be the garden of the kings, but now the park of El Retiro is for the people.

We sit down beside a small man-made lake. Francisco disappears. Massive stone pillars rise up out of the concrete steps behind me and form a large semicircular shape. Bigger pillars again in the middle of these and their job is to hold up an enormous greenish bronze-looking statue of a big man on a big horse who looks to have done big things with his life.

That's Alfonso, a voice from behind me explains, the young king of Spain.

Francisco stands there with two tiny glasses of beer in one hand and a paper cone of roasted chestnuts in the other. He places between us the paper cone and I let on I've eaten chestnuts before. I take one slightly slower than him and follow his lead. We bite and spit and chew and drink.

The beers are tiny.

Your father used to say that.

I nod in the statue's direction. I'd say Alfonso could do with one.

He was only sixteen when he became the king of Spain, but Alfonso himself was dead and in his grave for his twenty-seventh birthday.

My father's boyfriend Francisco goes on to tell me that he himself is third-generation Madrilenian, a rarity, a native, *un gato*, as the minority of natives are known. But then the tables are turned and he tells me about *my* life. That I was an only child but I was not spoilt. That I broke my small toe when I was eight. That I'd banged it off the bottom of the swimming pool the first time I was brought for a lesson. When I smell bleach, to this day, I feel phantom pains in my left little toe.

When he says this, I feel the phantom pains. I look away. I see clearly my father – the man, the grafter, the fighter, the leaver, the inserter of rage and creator of shame from silence, the ruiner of mantelpiece thoughts, the slayer of Jimmy Roundbale Delaney – jumping the barrier between seats and pool and diving in and lifting me out of the water and carrying me out the door to the car and to the hospital but, *No, first, we'll buy sweets, we need sweets, they'll take your mind off the pain, princess*, and I'd forgotten he used to call me that.

I'd forgotten that only after we bought the sweets did we go to the casualty department, both loaded up on sherbet straws and KP Choc Dips, and I'm not sure I've ever been so impressed by someone's decision-making skills – sweets first, then hospital. The sherbet straws worked like codeine. And the following month, despite my screams, my father throws me back into the pool. Sherbet sticks again on the way home.

I go quiet beside Francisco. I pick the box up from the bench and hold it against my chest. I pull it in tight. Francisco puts his arm around my shoulder. It is not awkward this time. I lean into him, briefly.

Why has he the hand out, your man Alfonso?

RESURRECTION
OF A CORNCRAKE

Burnt oil drains from the Belle cement mixer, bruising the earth below. It's where it came from.

The boy in you drove daily two donkeys up stoney Roscommon hills. A soggy pull off the ground no matter what time of year it was. Trees dotted at wayward angles. Some days there was no separation between you and animal – you'd nearly drive them with your hands in your pockets. The corncrakes' *crex crex* echoing all around. It was like their salute to the work.

A young girl watched you from the big gates. One of the McKeons – you knew by the eyes. She was Enda McKeon's youngest, Lily. The confidence just to stand there and look at another passing by. Head up. Inquisitive. Not a flinch. All kitted out in a little dress and shoes and it only a Thursday. Your home place up the hills had no gate. It be hard imagine staring out at passersby up there.

Enda McKeon's offer of paid labour was a good a reason as any to jack in national school. Landing in more often than not with one arm as long as the other, no sod of turf or lump of coal like the rest, it meant you always sat furthest away from the fire. McCrann only nineteen years old himself but he had an uncle on the board of education. His chair just got turned around one day and he was the new teacher. The McKeon kids close to filling the front row. Lily in the middle, a shoulder lower, fine head of ringlets. Looking straight up at McCrann with that same confident stare.

What else could be done only keep the head down and drive them two asses up through the world. Past McKeons' gate. Up by the milking sheds. Around by the last of the outhouses that marked the start of the ascent. When you reached the plateau where the big animals were summered and you were out of sight and the donkeys' load of feed dumped and graped into the trough, only then would you cede to the pull. Lie down on your back. A sky mesmeric once the clouds cleared, once the sun set. Nights were often spent up there wondering what it was that you were looking up at. What exactly was looking back down at you.

The oil still drains from the cement mixer. Lily is back at the kitchen window. Those hands that used cling to gates and watch you drive donkeys, they cling now to the stay of the casement window. They have lengthened and veined and wrinkled. Her ringlets have straightened. The hair is thin. Her two big toes are permanently crossed over her long toes whether she's wearing the tight shoes or not. She has developed an arsenal of head-shakes through the decades to get her points across to you from distance.

There was a certain head-shake for shipping a length of willow over a donkey's back. Something along the lines of *You cruel little bastard.* The shake as you chased corncrakes into hedgerows. The one she used when you used drink like a fool, when she could find you on your knees in the toilet. But that one there now – as she studies the ground below the mixer – there's a nuance to this head-shake you haven't seen before.

An illusion once took hold of you. Lil and yourself had just bought the 1.5-acre site and there was no rush with the build, the thinking. A caravan would do the finest for four or five years, but a tinny RTÉ voice snapped you out of it – Hurricane Charley is on his way from Florida. He'll hit the Sligo coast tomorrow, 25 August 1986, and the mood is not great. Expect massive rain, wild winds, torrential flooding.

You tied the caravan down as best you could with ratchet straps and blue rope and anchored everything to bales of 9-inch cavity blocks, cursing yourself all the while for not yet starting the plans, never mind the build. Lily shook back and forth inside the caravan with the wind. She shook for days after the storm passed. Charley the bastard, he blew a new sort of nervousness into her.

And the oil still drips and seeps, a lovely blue-black inking the soil. It's where it came from, Lil, you say over your shoulder when you hear the kitchen window open. The oil coming down in straight lines from the bottom of the engine. It's where it belongs, you tell her. Don't talk shite, man. Burnt oil won't make it back down to where it came from. You know it doesn't work like that. Fairy talk is all that is – you're polluting the place is what you're at. Plain and simple. Why aren't you using the catchment tray?

You watch her walk away into the shadows of the kitchen, but the Belle you continue to drain. Hands on you black from the work. Hands that know nothing only work. Hands that keep the machinations of the mind at bay.

An old man used come out to McKeons' from the town of Boyle and walk the hills while he waited for Clark's Bar to open. He could have been a Crow or a Candon, or a Smith. He had the height of a Smith. There was nothing figurative nor poetic in what he told you, he wanted to make that clear. It's just that that bogland down there was full of stories, crimes old and new, all fossilized within each and every sod of turf. That's why there's such a push to burn the stuff – to get rid of all the evidence.

It was impossible to imagine how the clothes he wore were ever took off. That tweed jacket smelt of everything necessary to live a life. The cooker, the fire, the bed, the toilet, the animals. His legs too frail to be reaching over and pulling up and down underpants and socks and trousers. But he still motored himself across large distances on that push bike. The two walking sticks balanced across the handlebars as he pedalled. And he would have known well back then his words were safe with you – a boy too young to cop what was really being said.

Tell them to bury me in that bog when I go. The eyes on him swollen as he telling you this out the side of his mouth, as if he didn't want the two donkeys to hear. I'll live forever that way.

There was nothing to say back. All you could do was imagine how you might get his crooked nose and wonky legs down into the sod.

Hurricane Charley's winds reached 65.2 mph, it was declared the day after the storm. Rainfall peaked at 280 mm, the greatest level ever recorded in the country. Over five hundred buildings inundated, two rivers burst their banks and crops throughout the country destroyed. Eleven people lost their lives to Charley – he drowned four in flooded waters and gave another a heart attack while being evacuated. But what Charley was actually saying was that you needed a trade, you needed steady money. Ideally, you'd want to stop the bolloxing and get the foundation down for you and Lil. And above all, get your own cement mixer and stop borrowing that heap of shite from Tom Joe.

The Belle she was bought at the end of '86 from the plant men over in Tulsk. The envelope of twenty-pound notes stuffed between your legs as you drove over to collect it. Gazing at the mixer's newness in the rear-view mirror on the way home. Foundations were planned as you drove slow through Knocknafushoga. Concrete over lengths of mild steel, a mix of 1:1:2. You heard the cement and sand and aggregate already turning over inside her long before you first spun the starter handle. You saw the house built before a block was laid.

When the start was made, you thumbed a sign of the cross into the first trowel of wet mortar before the initial 9-inch cavity went down. It was an act the father did before you, although he did it his way, with hay. He would take two wisps, straighten them out, then cross them over each other and place them on the ground where the summer's first cock was to be built.

Subcontracting out some of the work, that was Lil's call. The meitheal long dead and buried. Cash in hand or no show. And Lil, did she fuck trust you with the electrics. It be hard blame her. Only for you were both up on rubber tyres in that caravan, the extra socket you wired in for her hairdryer would have ended her on the spot. She still gets the phantom jolts the odd time she passes by a hairdresser's.

You lined up Emmet Lennon for cables and sockets and power boards. Young Joe Naughton gave you a dig out with the pipes. The Hynes man with the jeep raised the roof with you, a man who has since passed. The guts of the second fixings you did yourself.

It was the corncrake used signal to farmers when the hay was ready be cut. Directing the work from one field to the next with its call, the bird a class of avian foreman. The father and his neighbours would take heed and go to the fields with scythes and pitchforks, slicing close to but just over whatever ground nesters they came across. Eggs would already be hatched by then. Mother birds could vacate their young if needed.

Oh we've always had corncrakes on the brain, the Smith man claimed in his ever-confessional drone. You both scanning Enda McKeon's low field behind the outhouses at the time, trying to find the source of a *crex crex* that had persisted for days without a single sighting. And Lily McKeon still standing at the gates. So fixated on you that the Smith man might as well have been a ghost.

The ancients were no different, Smith nodding to the land as he spoke. Such was the want on them to have them fucken birds close, they'd have the audacity to deny their absence during winter. The corncrake is gone nowhere, is what they would say to each other. It's just transformed itself into the common moorhen. For the cold and the like. Look at them all out there on the lake. Fighting over rats and eggs.

Rummaging in his pockets another day, the Smith man told you this next one – It's why I eat them. To see can I break the hold they have on us. But the more I think on the old stories, the more I understand the madness.

The Belle kept her colour those first twelve months of work. But site to site, her body began lose its shiny complexion to a light film of mortar. And the mortar got speckled with lime and scud, screed and skim-coat, joint filler and bonding. The same materials that marked and pocked your face and overalls and body after each and every day's work above on the 8-foot planks.

You had power in those days to scale lifts of scaffolding without a ladder to save time. You could read the need of a ceiling. When a ferocious shower of rain pulled a gable end's worth of fresh mortar to the ground, you could stare the same rain down, as if to say, I will not be bested by any system of weather. When that gable was recoated, levelled, second-coated, napped, safely dried – it was a feeling that lasted all evening. It triggered great sleep.

Steel, mortar, wheelbarrow ramps, makeshift bucket pulley systems, there was calmness in the noise of a site, in the clash of materials, in the sudden uproar of Kango hammers and circular saws and the unexpected bouts of silence when all tradesmen on site simultaneously stopped, as if conducted to do so. These periods sometimes caught you off guard. You could find yourself reflecting on lime-burnt hands, wet socks, an aching back. The same sandwich and the same digestives in the same poxy Jacob's USA biscuit tin from how many Christmases ago? Why in the name of Christ have you spent the majority of your life hacking and hammering and dogging yourself, from the age of eleven until now? You know men who stayed in school and worked as clerks. They put on clean clothes in the morning. They drank tea from cups without oil stains. Their sandwiches never tasted of limestone. It's fairly doubtful they ever boiled up a kettle in the back of a Hiace while sitting on a spare tyre amidst a torrent of rain. Too wet even to open the side door and let some fumes of gas escape.

But the reflections wouldn't hold. A hammer would drop, a drill would spin, you'd scrape the hawk clean and brush the remaining dirt into the wash bucket and then scoop out a fresh hawkful from the wheelbarrow and go back to humming the same two lines from the tune stuck in your head. There was a knowing come evening when you saw them other men in the rear-view mirror at a traffic lights on the way home – in a way you'd won.

Your body got what it required. Your mind thought of nothing only the spud. Your forehead wasn't scrunched.

The way a wall took a wetting in the morning said a lot about the day ahead. The sound of rocks sloshing around in the cement mixer on a Monday evening when the morning hangover had close to crucified you, it was the sound of a small miracle. One of only two plasterers in the county who could cut and shape cornerstones freehand, you were never out of work. Some looking in might have gotten the impression there was a bit of an artist at play. The way you'd stand back to admire a freshly skimmed and trowelled ceiling of an evening, the winter dark coming in around you. A work-light in the corner throwing theatrical shadows onto bare plaster-board walls as you walked closer to and backed away from the work. The last wet patches hardening into something permanent. The body throbbing with a want to sit down but you'd be gripped by the need to sprinkle a drop of water up over your head and give the ceiling one more lick. Each stroke would be delivered as delicate or as hard as required. And the daytime cacophony of mixers and drills and traffic, of chat and radio and footsteps. Of agricultural engines and the animals they fed. All these sounds now fading with the light and all that was left was the tap dripping outside the window and the distant hum of machinery retreating from fields and the sound of the last few scrapes of your trowel. The newly skimmed ceiling completely smooth and jointless, like it had come into the universe as such.

There was a bit of an artist in you, alright. But a trade is a trade, nothing more, is what you would probably say to that.

No different to plenty of people you know, machines develop unusual characters over time. To get the Belle going these fresh mornings, intention and technique is as crucial as gaskets and pistons. A certain stance is needed so as not to aggravate the hip or the knee. It's all about how you hold your mouth, a young labourer told you once.

The original metal wheels you removed as a young man by raising the upper body from its axle and welding it down onto the chassis of a rubber-tyre trailer. The only way to convince people the mixer was once yellow is to squat them down to the tiny patch where the mortar never took. A 1970s Lister engine in her. Its single cylinder owing nothing to no one. A light board attached but never wired right. On dark winter drives home only a hi-vis jacket flapping from the rear and somehow you were never pulled.

She's ended up a unique-looking contraption, the Belle, something that has been cared for, but the care has been rough – dog rough.

The old man who might have been a Smith came back another day and took you by the arm to show you how to trap a corncrake and not be fooled by its antics. How to read the thrown voice and find its nesting eggs. He shuffled all the way behind you and the two donkeys up to the high field. Making careful not to land his sticks or feet on any of the rounded rocks that jutted from the ground like bald ossified heads. He stopped for regular breaks, letting on he was examining a tuft of reeds, flipping over a dried cow pat, uprooting the smaller of the rocks. You wouldn't know what you'd find.

He had land once, a long way back. But he sold it on to one of the music people in Gurteen. He shook his head mid-sentence and said no more about it.

The cows grazed on the feed and the donkeys stood close to the wall the far side, looking back down on where they came from. The Smith man's shaking hands disappeared into his coat pockets and came out with a bottle and a newspaper package.

A drop of tea each and from the opened newspaper he offered you some meat. He said it was no sin.

This townland is alive with corncrakes – they'd only take over the place if some sort of culling wasn't to happen. The Celts used eat them in stews beside Lough Gur a thousand year ago. What's good for the goose is good for the gander. There's nothing special about that bird. Ate away, boy.

The days that followed you went quiet inside yourself. The two asses even sussed you were off and kept their distance. Looking back, it could nearly be categorized as a period of melancholy. A twisted learning you never looked for. Six months or a year since you began your first paid labouring job for Enda McKeon. Since your schooling finished. Since you could afford the first pair of shoes. Lily McKeon's big eyes, big like all the McKeon women before her. It pained the most when she looked over and you couldn't bring yourself to look back. You had silenced a bird.

When you silence a bird the sound follows you. It can still be heard now, all over the country. Age-wise – you'd have to put at least fifteen on yourself by the time you started to cut hay for the McKeons. A finger-bar mower on a Massey 365. The hay was to be cut in June, a timing that meant the corncrakes' eggs would be hatched. You drove the Massey plenty slow to give the mothers time to get their broods of jet-black hatchlings to the outskirts of the field, to that one yard of sanctuary along the stone wall where the finger-bar couldn't reach.

Cutting silage is the new thing, Enda McKeon declared a handful of summers later. McKeon had a way of always being in his work clothes but never being dirty. He had the wax jacket and the cord trousers and the wellington boots, but truth be told, if he kicked off the boots and put on a pair of shoes, he'd make it into most churches in the county without ever turning a head. He'd kept all his hair, not like your crowd. He never even paled that much during a drought of sun. You could never imagine him having to rush the breakfast. And for this silage crossover, he needed a pilot he could trust. First-cut May. Second-cut August. Nitrogen. Phosphorous. Potash. It's all about growth and yield. You nodded as if you were in agreement.

The corncrakes would be nesting in those fields at that time of year. They wouldn't be able to move their eggs, nor would they leave their nests unattended. How these statements of fact never made it out beyond your own skin, it's not an easy one to fathom. The big machines had you lured in – it could be that. In a way you worked for them as much as McKeon. The new John Deere. The shiny disc mower angled out behind it. There was something about them big machines. Their stillness as you stood beside them in otherwise desolate fields. The way they roared to life at the turn of a key. How they translated the workings of a mind onto land.

With the Belle mixer you left pebble-dashed dormer bungalows dotted around the townlands of the county. You left cornerstoned two-storeys. Wet-dashed cottages. Nap-finished garden walls.

With Enda McKeon's disc mower you left little to brag about. Walking them fields, hands behind the back after the first cut of silage. A bright May day. The disc mower's counter knives having sliced through everything you'd driven them over. The stomach telling you all you needed to know before your eyes clocked a thing, but the evidence was everywhere. The remains of the corncrakes and their nests and their young, scattered across the meadow like black pepper on cabbage.

You knew years earlier just sitting there with the two asses lying a distance from you and the corncrake in your belly. The ancients knew it well a millennia ago and they stuffing themselves beside Lough Gur. You knew at fifteen before you started that John Deere. You know now.

What are we talking since retirement was first attempted? It's ten years if it's a day. You take to choir singing. You take to nature documentaries. A BBC voice narrates the corncrake's annual migration from the British Isles to the Congo. Six thousand miles and the journey takes weeks. If a corncrake lives a full life, it will have spent a third of it suspended in flight. You spend a third of yours flat out in the bed.

By taking out those birds in that field with McKeon's disc mower, how many did you take out in total? In the long run, like? Wouldn't someone else have done it anyways if you hadn't? What does it fucking matter – it's only a bird isn't it? Some stupid bird with no brain worth talking about.

But brain enough to fool you all the same. Brain enough to make sounds you still long to hear at night, long before dreams come your way, and when you do hear it, you know the *crex crex* left the bird's throat fifty years back. It's been stuck in a memory ever since.

That fancy fuck of a BBC voice on about species extirpation and the oncoming mass extinctions – it's full of shite. You take to bird-spotting, they have to be out there somewhere. Nikon Monarch binoculars. Lil makes the sandwiches and you head north, you head west. Malin Head, Fanad Head. Omey Island, Turbot Island. But not one solitary corncrake.

At night in the B&B beside the pub overlooking Omey Island, you tell Lil things you've never uttered before. The first day you tried to trap a corncrake, you realized it was dead as you neared it. It lay completely lifeless, no movement in the belly or the open eyes. You turned away and looked back a moment later and it had tricked you. It was flying away.

How could they be that intelligent, Lil? I'm no bird man but I saw something in that corncrake. It knew it'd gotten one over on me. What's the difference between me and that bird anyhow? Apart from the fact the bird can fly away once it has enough.

In Scotland it is known as the blessed animal. The Scots too were migration deniers. It quietens itself, the corncrake, they say, and lies motionless every winter. Too still to be seen. Like one of them monks that used retreat out to the islands, trying to figure out the workings of himself.

Could we chance thinking the corncrakes are at the same thing now, Lil, just all year around?

When you realize she's asleep beside you, the feeling is you've gotten away with something. Because if you start to treat a marriage like a confessional box, the Smith man with the big limbs used say, you'll end up in the confessional box on your own. He spoke some amount of shite, that Smith man, but like the monkey at the typewriter, he got some things spot on.

To lay down fully this hawk and trowel, it seems too much. Seems like madness. Stopping for the sake of stopping because that's what happens at this age? There's plenty younger than you being put into homes, and those men and women have ailments that come from a stagnant body. The minds on them gone to seed.

The Nikon binoculars you can't even find anymore, but you picked up a new sponge float and an alloy hawk in Joe Simon's last week with your pension. There was change enough out of a fifty for a bag of lime. Only a bollox would have left them behind for that money.

There is a longing for circus acts on wind-rocked scaffolding, and although you haven't the knees or the shoulders or the eyes, you'll take what you can get. You took on too much a while back – a full house in town – and you had to subcontract it out to the two brothers from Frenchpark. Tight operators. It's the first job you couldn't finish.

Thank God, is all that's to be said, for the nixer. For the community of people who come to you when the job is small enough. Who bring you in and feed you and leave out the sandwiches and the apple tarts when they can't personally attend you.

Thank God for the walls that can be knocked around the yard and rebuilt. For that body of yours that hasn't refused you a day yet. The more time spent on the go, the less time alone in a chair with your rights and your wrongs.

There's still fucken time, Lil, is there not? But her mouth sags more. And even when her eyes are open, it be hard claim you both ever inhabit the same world.

All that mattered once, it happened on those Roscommon hills. In the grind of driving the same two asses up the same hill, and going at it again the next day and the next, but never getting that feeling you achieved what you set out to do.

There was a contentment in the eyes of the animals you drove. They could focus straight ahead and not get distracted. What it must be like to have no great want beyond the basics. You rest your hand on Lil's arm as you listen to her dreaming. It stops you floating out the window.

Your own dream when it comes is of a pair of donkeys tumbling slow through the air. They catch fire as you look up at them, only their dust making it to the ground. It falls over you in the bed like industrial ash. In the morning it will be gone. The light will have melted it.

To resurrect a corncrake, rub the teeth of a comb over the edge of a matchbox. Rub the comb slow, the matchbox closed and full. Do this for two or three days, or as long as the symptoms persist.

The sound you learned to make with the comb and the matchbox, it was indistinguishable from the real thing. You would put the corncrake back in your pocket once the donkeys were ready to work again.

ENDSONG

I

We sleep under the hood of the Red Giant. Its warm diesel engine. The low sound of the distant sea. Island comings and goings. We let it all in.

The Red Giant has MF 165 etched into its hood. People come and go, say, *The Massey Ferguson's a solid beast. Blood red. A chugger.*

From the window of their bothy, the fat one and the quiet one scatter carrot tops and bottoms. Bread crusts. Fish spines on Fridays. Meat grinds on Sundays. Potato skin. Lamb fat. Chicken bone. Rabbit eye. Pig ear. Bottle tops of milk they pull from the goat. Goat rib. Goat heart. *The fucking birds need dinner too.*

To keep food in our bellies, we watch over the Red Giant at night. We watch over them in their bothy. That they may wake and work in the morning.

Once, as the centre of the sky blackened – and around its edges we saw amethyst and lavender, indigo and onyx, and a hundred other shades of purple that we've never heard them name, like the purple that glows around dying flowers – the bad man came. *Pit pat pit pat pit pat.* Stop. Boots off, slung over his shoulder. The *pit pat pit pat* gone. He had his own wind that exploded from his insides. Fire and gas and rotten eggs. When right beside us – he didn't see us, his face disfigured in new-moon dark, his breathing lightest as his hand went for the bothy door – we sang. We sang violent song. Rhythmless and patternless. Sharp and pointed. Bullets and knives. We sang machine guns from the movies they watch in the bothy. The fists and kicks from the cowboy punch-ups. The chop and slice of the goat on the table. The fat one and the quiet one woke, heads out the window. *Run you rotten drunk fuck, run. You wouldn't rob air.* Like this we watch over them.

When the Red Giant won't sing a note, the fat one's face swells up and goes red. *Fuck of a tractor. Fuck of a tractor. A rotten Massey bastard Ferguson. It'll be John Deere for me around here. You'll sit here and rust, you fuck. John Deere around here. The starlings won't even piss on you. Fuck of a tractor.*

The quiet one arrives to help. *What's wrong, a mhacín?* They call each other *a mhacín*. It comes from a song they used to sing but now that song is gone. *Why are you shouting, a mhacín? Don't you know it's only a spark plug or a drop of dirty diesel?*

Their singing turns to squabble and huffing and *tut tut tut*. The fat one's face swells up into a storm. *Hok*, spit. The quiet one goes quiet. They pull out their pipes and tinker with the charred walls of the chambers. *Tap tap tap* the scrapings onto a rock. With care they place fresh tobacco into their bowls, mounding it high – *pap pap* to a steady draw. They breathe smoke out from their bellies. It rises up. We let it in. We let it in.

When the wind blows, we rock a little on the power lines and fence tops and branches. When the smoke sits deep within them, deep within us, we watch them walk over and peek into where we like to sleep, especially on the cold nights. The fat one looks and scratches, the quiet one points and twists. Turning their heads sideways and holding a long stick up to the sun. *She's OK for oil, a mhacín.*

The fat one shakes his head. *Roll on death till I get a rest.* The quiet one tinkers with the Red Giant's steel heart, iron lungs, wheezy windpipes. The fat one climbs up onto the big seat, pushes with his feet and turns with his hands and *fucks* and *cunts* and *not one more bastardin' second* and *nothing good ever came out of that Massey Ferguson factory.* The quiet one looks up. Doesn't *fuck*. Doesn't *cunt*. Drops of water on his face. His hands black in the Red Giant's guts. *Did you drain her? I did. Bleed her? I did. Reseat the plugs? I didn't.*

And between the spinning and the tinkering and the cursing and the bleeding, the Red Giant comes to life.

> *thud, th thud, th thud, th thud, th thud*
> *th th th th th th th th th th th th th th th*

We close all our eyes. We sing along.

II

We sleep under the hood of the Red Giant, beside the headless bothy. The rooftops by the shore sticking up out of the water like a fleet of capsized boats. Their chimneys taking in breaths for the people below, living their underwater lives.

The Red Giant's hood is holed with rust. The rain it lets in, when it comes, when it *tap tap tap*s, *ta ta ta*, it cools us down. When it doesn't come, when the heat stops sleep, when the Red Giant's tyres hold their hot all night, we sing. We sing until all the mouths on the island are singing. We sing until the rain comes again.

Some songs are long and heavy and take all our energy – they come from the elders. The elders sing us our past. They sing the Red Giant's *th th th th*. *Thud th thud th thud th thud*. They sing the men who fed them. The frost and ice that used to winter the place. The sounds that came from the roof that once sat on the bothy. The old sea when it sang far away.

When one of their songs stops working, when it stops giving us what we need, we *inspect. Tinker. Turn. Twist.* We change it into a new song. A new song is like the old one only it works better. We hear the *tap tap tap* of the rain on the hood. Like this we know the song is working.

To see a lapwing, we sing *pea-wit, pea-wit, pea-wit*. We sing it again. We wait. To lure in the curlew, we bubble out their call. We wait for the long wading legs. The down-curved bills. Brown streaky plumage. To call in the wood pigeon, *wou-rook too, coo-oou, wo-wou rook too, coo-oou*, and we will hear the slapping of wing tips and the upswing of their flap.

But the Red Giant's song we sing the most. *Thud th thud th thud th thud. Th th th th th th.* Sometimes from inside the bothy. Perched up on the bones of the armchairs. Chanting it all through the night.

III

We sleep under the hood of the Red Giant, beside the rubble from the bothy. We rummage odds and ends. Sticks and bricks and bones. We peek and preen. Perch and pant and dive. Dig and look in the soil. We *pit pat pit pat.* Our marks in the dust. The ground below the dust hard like rock. We dwindle. *The fucking birds need dinner too. The fucking birds. Fuck of a bird.* The ground is black. The soil is dead. The air tastes like well-smoked pipes.

Sitting inside the engine, lining up on the hot pipe, shuffle shuffle side to side to stop our feet from flaming. We try shelter from the heart-red flames of the sky. We try hear how it all is, but the sea's all there is to be heard. *Swish* and *swoosh.* All day long. *Swish, swoosh.* The *swish* and the *swoosh.* The sky red above and the earth black below, a screaming in our bellies, we peck and clutch, but the earth is as empty as us. The blood sky finds us no matter where we hide. Sometimes we kill.

Sometimes we kill when our eyes are swollen. We spike out our head feathers. Our beaks sharp. We leave them on the pile of rubble and just watch them. We only kill what is smaller than us. Kestrels. Purple martins. Bluebirds. Woodpeckers. Sometimes we watch them a full day, in case they are pretending death. Then we'll eat them. We'll eat their young. We'll eat their eggs. Like this we'll survive.

IV

We sleep under the hood of the Red Giant. The warm salty water slaps and mouths at its wheels. The rust the dirt the moss. The *swish* and the *swoosh*. We *pit pat* to the water, we look back up at ourselves. We don't see us in the sky. The power that guided our patterns of flight, it no longer works like it should. It got broke like the Red Giant. Broke like the soil. *Fuck of a sky*. Fuck of a sky.

To circle is all we do. We circle and circle, like we're stringed to the island itself. We splay our wings. We wrench. Swoop and rise. But circle and wait, circle and wait. The slice of wing through air. *Dirty air. Fuck of an air.* We can't leave. The markers that told us where to go are gone. The sea drank them. *Fuck of a sea.* There's nowhere to go. A mound of flies land close.

Metallic violet in the distance.

African violet at night.

Sky flames in the morning.

The flies in our bellies – we feel their wings move and scrape our insides.

Some of us drop out of the sky. We die as we fall, looking up. We die before the flies in our bellies. We watch ourselves dead in the dust.

We sing.

We sing the song of the last lapwing. We watched as it became the rubble. On top of the bones of the elders. On top of the bricks of the bothy. Held together by the dust of the workers.

We sing the song of the last curlew. The bubbly two-note call in its mouth. It disappeared for good.

We sing the song of the last people. The *um chhh um chhh um chhh* song they sang for days, dancing together in the trees at the very top of the island. The one who came down to see us after the *um chhh um chhh um chhh* song was over. Her blue roped hair. Her see-through face. Her legs long like the curlew.

Beside us she preened the dry skin from her bare feet. She didn't sing to start. She took out her glass pipe and smoked then sang for hours. *Don't worry.* That was one of her big songs. Over and over. *Don't worry. Everything's going to be fine.* Her voice perched high in the air. *Is it true all birds want sky burials? Is there anything I can do for you before I go back home?* She pointed at the air in front of her. *Look. Newborn glaciers. How cute.*

She held her face too close to us. Rubbing her eyes to see ours better. *I see my reflection. I see myself there. I'm already in you.* Inspecting her hands. *It's all about light. And colour. How light reflects what we see. Look. More new glaciers. This water will make its way back down to the shore. There. That's where the new glaciers will get born. They'll suck all this water up. All this madness. They'll suck it all up like a hoover. The new ice will shine. It will send the sun back home. It will put manners on it. And our home will right itself again. We'll all live in peace and comfort. Just wait and see. We have people working on it. Like them men up there, spraying the sky with sulphur to keep us cool.*

She took out her book. *Blessed is the one who reads aloud. Blessed are those who hear.*

She lay on her side. We heard her sleep and watched her slightly open eye. We sat on her chest. We preened her hair and jumper. *Tap tap tap* on her skull. She woke. Her pupils small. She didn't look at us. Her mouth was dust and dirt and her tongue black and her lips stuck together, keeping her quiet. She crawled. Laid herself down beside the Red Giant. The *swish* and the *swoosh*. *I can see you.*

Her face the white around old animal tracks.

Her face the white of nothing left inside.

Her mouth fell open, she made loud sleep sounds. *Pit pat pit pat pit pat.* We perched on the bridge of her nose. We balanced on the ledges of her eyes. We swarmed her arms and chest and belly and rose up and down with her breaths. We lined her legs and covered her bare flaking feet. The last of us picked between her teeth. Some blood came from her gums and we picked and pecked all the more. We watched our eyes bulge from the drink. More.

Her arms rose and her legs kicked, our weight kept them down. We closed her eyes over and her mouth over and her over with more of us. And more of us came and covered her again. And again. And more of us. Until her chest stopped rising and stopped falling. We sang her as she went.

ACKNOWLEDGMENTS

Thanks to:

Bolorchimeg Dashdorj
The family
Brendan Duffin
Miguel Alvarez Rodriguez
Terry Craven and Desperate Literature
Gary Robertson
Martin Tivnan
Martin Kelleher
John O'Hare
Connor Shine and Avery Rowan
Danielle McLaughlin
Lisa McInerney and *The Stinging Fly*
Owen Murphy
Seán Farrell, Antony Farrell, and everyone who
works at The Lilliput Press
The Arts Council
Margot, Travis, and Andy